American Dreaming
and Other Stories

American Dreaming
and Other Stories

Doris Iarovici

NOVELLO PRESS

CHARLOTTE 2005

Published in the United States by

Novello Festival Press, Charlotte, North Carolina.

This is a work of fiction and any resemblance to real persons
or events is purely coincidental.

Library of Congress Cataloging-in-Publication Data

Iarovici, Doris.

 American dreaming and other stories / Doris Iarovici.

  p.   cm.

 ISBN 0-9760963-4-X

 1. United States—Social life and customs—Fiction.   I. Title.

 PS3609.A76A84 2004

 813'.6—dc22

                                        2005016292

"Facts" appeared in *Crab Orchard Review,* Winter 2002

"If Wishes Were Horses" appeared in *Crescent Review,* Fall 1993

Printed in the United States of America

Book design by Jacky Woolsey

First Edition

To Marius and Mioara Iarovici
Whose courage to start anew made everything possible

And to Larry Katz
Who believed from the start and made the possible real

Contents

Facts

*B*efore she was ever born, Lisa's parents had a major philosophical difference. This difference kept them from getting married in the first place. Lisa's mother, Shelly, wanted children, while Bruce, her father, did not. Shelly never failed to point out that Bruce had been honest and up front about this. He'd told Shelly on their second date about the mental illness he did not want to pass on to a child. Shelly understood; Shelly agreed. But for her everything changed with the first unexpected bouts of morning sickness late in her thirty-eighth year.

When her mother spoke to Lisa about her father, her voice softened and her eyes drifted beyond Lisa's right shoulder, up, to a point far away. Sometimes a dreamy smile played on her lips. Hearing about Bruce as a four, five, six-year-old, Lisa would be filled with a nose-pricking yearning for the tall man with the long black hair pulled into a ponytail whom she knew from the three-by-five photo in the heart-shaped ceramic frame on her dresser. But by the time she was eleven, twelve, a hammering fury filled her chest at the mention of Bruce's name. So began her campaign to prove he didn't matter in her life. She'd cut her mother short when his name came up, leave the room, curse him. By the time Lisa was fourteen, she had won. Shelly no longer talked about Bruce. And Lisa made sure no one else in her life knew he existed.

Yet here she was being taken to meet him.

Curled in the passenger seat of Gabe's Honda Civic, going seventy up Interstate 95, Lisa kept her icy hands tucked into her armpits. The flash cards she'd made the night before, index cards covered with microbiology facts she needed to memorize by Monday, lay untouched, rubberbanded on her lap.

"Hungry?" Gabe said, flicking his eyes from the road to Lisa. She jumped, drawing a sharp breath.

"Oh—sorry," he said, smiling with a bewildered frown. "I just thought you might be hungry by now. You skipped breakfast. I packed you an egg sandwich on an English muffin."

"You're so sweet."

"And there's a carton of orange juice in the cooler, by your feet."

She blinked and noticed the red-and-white container for the first time.

"I'm not hungry, but thanks."

"Maybe you should eat a little anyway. You know how you get when you skip meals."

She turned toward the loblolly pines flying past her window so he wouldn't notice her roll her eyes, but at the same time she told herself, *He's right. You do get bitchy when you're hungry—he's only stating a fact.* Turning back toward him, she noticed that instead of his usual flannel shirt over a tee, he wore a denim button-down tucked neatly into black jeans. His dark curls were flattened and slightly frizzy, meaning he'd run a brush across them. She skimmed his cheek with her fingertips.

"You shaved."

A smile flickered across his red lips: the reddest lips she'd ever seen on a guy. Sometimes for a split second she felt the urge to turn her face as his came toward her for a kiss—but of course she didn't.

She kissed with her eyes closed.

"I shaved in honor of meeting your dad," Gabe said.

"I wish you wouldn't call him that."

"But it's a fact. That's who he is."

"Oh—I thought a dad was someone who did more than donate sperm and disappear," she said, then bit her lower lip.

"Leese. We're mending fences, remember?"

"There's nothing to mend, really. My mother didn't need him. I was fine without him."

"That's what you've said."

"It's true."

Facts. Normally facts were her friends, so why was nausea rising into her throat? Gabe was humming along with a Dead song on one of his CDs. This was just an ordinary conversation to him. He glanced at her, his brow smooth and his green eyes completely unperturbed, and winked. The nausea in her throat tightened into a knot and she couldn't speak. *You can't argue with facts,* she told herself. Not that she and Gabe argued. Hadn't they compared facts about what they each wanted out of life as carefully as computers match answer keys to bubble sheets? Hadn't they both said, three kids, a house with a huge yard out in the country, a stay-at-home parent—with Gabe agreeing to play that part?

"I've never been the ambitious type, into the rat-race thing," Gabe told her on their first date.

"That's pretty refreshing," she'd said, laughing. "Now my turn," and then her mouth went parched and she swallowed. She recited: "My friends might say I *am* into the rat-race thing—that I'm a workaholic—but they don't know that I go to Wellspring to get special ingredients to cook up special dinners Friday nights. But, um—then again, sometimes I worry that I got into med school by mistake—that I can't possibly belong there. That they'll figure it out and send me packing. So I work really hard to make sure that never happens."

Gabe's forehead had remained smooth, and the languorous smile that had trickled across his lips hadn't wavered. He'd watched her with his face slightly upturned and his eyes narrowed, as if savoring a glass of good wine. She cleared her throat and kept talking, her words spilling out faster and faster.

"And . . . let's see, more dirt on me. More dirt. I'm a restless sleeper. I kick without meaning to." She'd flushed and turned her eyes to her lap. "And . . . ah. Ready for the big one? I've never told a guy this. My, um, parents, were not married. My mom is a sixties throw-back, a space cadet but an absolute sweetheart. My father did not want me to be born." She'd looked back up at Gabe. "He's crazy—"

"He'd have to be, to not want—"

"No, I mean *crazy,* really—please let me finish. Certifiable. He's been hospitalized a bunch of times. So far I haven't had any break-downs but I'm still young—it could happen. Like a—time bomb. Not that any of it matters to me—but you should know, if . . ."

She'd locked her eyes onto his placid ones, thinking, O.K., leave now, go ahead, I can take it. I don't need a guy and never have. But his eyes didn't widen, and his face didn't flush. He reached across the

Facts

....

5

table and stroked her cheek with the backs of his first and middle fingers.

"Is that *all* the dirt?" he'd said, eyes twinkling, the dimple in his cheek deepening, and Lisa's chest had expanded with elation and she'd grabbed his hand and kissed the square knuckles, and they'd gone back to his place and made love quietly in the bedroom while his roommate watched "Who Wants to be a Millionaire?" in the next room.

Gabe moved into her place two weeks later.

They hit D.C. around ten, and sailed through without any traffic. In the same way that he planned their dates and was planning their wedding, Gabe had arranged their entire drive to avoid major city rush hours. Lisa ate her egg sandwich and drank Tropicana straight from the carton, not noticing the flowered Dixie cups Gabe had stacked next to the cooler.

She began to flip through her microbiology cards. *Shigellae: gram-negative rods. Ferment glucose but not lactose.* Lactose.

"I forgot to tell you I had colic as an infant," she said, not looking up and continuing to flip cards.

"*What?*"

"You know. When I was giving you the facts. On me. I left out colic."

"You poor thing."

She cast a rapid glance at him but there was no sarcasm in his expression.

"It's not like I remember it or anything. Must've been hard on my mom. You know, having a baby that doesn't shut up for a minute.

Who knows—maybe I cried and cried when—Bruce—met me too. Maybe he thought it was a sign—of mental illness."

Gabe's eyes darted to Lisa, and back to the road.

"Leese, tell me you're not worrying about what he'll think of you. You know he's going to love you. You're the perfect daughter. Beautiful, smart, accomplished. It's going to be really neat, getting together. Finally getting closure."

"*Closure?*"

He smiled.

"Hey, I took two semesters' worth of psych!"

"I don't know." She decided now was not the time to tell him how she always kept an eye on herself—for signs. Not that she thought Bruce was right about her—but still. The possibility filled her veins with ice. She worked hard to not let herself get too angry, or too loud, or too sad—or even too happy.

"Lisa, man. Duke Medical School . . . really, what more could any father want? You know how psyched *my* parents are about it."

Lisa wanted to say that was the whole point; that Bruce should not get to meet her *now,* when she was a *somebody,* if he never wanted to meet her as a regular kid. But Gabe seemed so excited. His eyes shone and he drummed his hands against the steering wheel in rhythm with the Dead. She kept her thoughts to herself.

Lisa had never been to Queens. As the highway fed into narrower congested roads and Gabe thrust maps into her lap, she bent all her thoughts to matching the map with the street signs, and with the yellow Post-It with Sarah's directions. Her hands began to warm, color returning to her fingernails. She hardly noticed the red brick buildings pressing in on them. Traffic lights blinked from green to yellow to red so rapidly that several times, they found themselves midway through an intersection against the light. Finally, they were on a narrow street lined with small houses that looked so similar, Lisa wondered if people accidentally wandered through their neighbors' door at the end of the day. Gradually she picked out small differences here and there: a screened-in porch instead of a patio. Stucco or vinyl siding instead of bricks. Gabe slowed the Honda, and painstakingly maneuvered into a very tight parking place.

Lisa took a deep breath and stepped out of the car. Her right leg tingled from having been tucked underneath her the last half hour, and she shook it out and winced as she put weight on it. Gabe sprang around the front of the car and put an arm around her, giving her shoulder a squeeze.

"Ready?" he asked.

"I'm fine," she said, surprised because it was true. "I don't really feel a thing. It's like I'm watching myself approach the house, watching myself touch the buzzer—"

But before she could finish her sentence, the paneled glass door of number 68-39 opened and then the white wood door behind that swung back, and out came a middle-aged woman, slightly plump, with short red-brown hair. She wore a navy cotton dress that Lisa recognized as Land's End, and a beige-and-navy silk scarf knotted around her neck like a flight attendant's.

"Lisa?" she called. "Welcome, welcome Lisa! I'm Sarah—we spoke when you called?" To Gabe she called, "I'm Sarah, Bruce's wife. Please, please come in!" The woman's bright green eyes crinkled in a warm smile, and she stepped into the house while holding the screen door open with one arm and beckoning to Lisa and Gabe with the other. Lisa noticed that Sarah was plumper and taller than her mother, better dressed, and younger-seeming. But as she stepped closer, she could make out the web of fine lines around her eyes, as well as a deep groove just above her eyebrows into which some makeup had caked.

Lisa stepped through the door as if she were leaving a dock for a canoe. The door led directly into a small living room crowded with fading furniture and stacked with books. There were bookshelves built into the walls across from the sofa, bookshelves on the wall beside the front door, and then more books piled on the end tables beside the sofa, and in stacks on the floor beside the chairs. Abstract oil paintings with heavy brush strokes adorned the book-free areas of wall. The coffee table was set with a tray of Milano cookies, cut vegetables and dip, and four empty glasses. As they handed their coats to Sarah, Lisa's eyes scanned the empty room. She let her breath out through pursed lips, then froze when in the next moment a tall man strode in from the back of the house.

He wore a black long-sleeved T-shirt with faded jeans, and his hair was thin and gray but still pulled away from his face in a skinny ponytail that dangled down his back. The skin on his face hung loosely and his mouth curled down at the edges. Lisa noticed that his hands were trembling. His black eyes darted from Sarah to Lisa, and then rested on Gabe.

"Who's he?" were his first words. His voice was gruff. Lisa felt a stab of disappointment.

"Bruce, this is Lisa, and—" Sarah began, her own voice even and calm, but he cut her off.

"I know who she is. Looks just like Shelly did, years ago. But who the devil's he?"

"Gabe Sutter," Lisa said, finding her voice. "My fiancé."

"Nice to meet you, sir," Gabe said, extending his right hand, which Bruce gripped firmly after an awkward moment's hesitation.

"What's he doing here?" Bruce asked Sarah.

"Why don't we all sit down?" Sarah motioned to the sofa. "I'll make some herbal tea."

"You can offer them coffee. *They're* not on lithium, they can have it," Bruce barked, and Lisa noticed Sarah's nostrils flare momentarily.

"I'd love some coffee, thanks," Gabe said. He sank into the sofa and stretched his arm along its back. "It was a long drive. I thought I might drop off several times."

"Thought you said she was going to be in town," Bruce said to Sarah, who gave an insouciant shrug and disappeared into the kitchen. He was still standing, as was Lisa, who suddenly found it difficult to move. He frowned at Lisa. "Thought she said you said you were going to be in town. You didn't make a special trip just to see me, did you?"

Lisa swallowed, and glanced at Gabe. He had helped himself to a cookie and looked as if he were settling in to watch a football game.

"In fact, it was Gabe's idea to—ah—give a call," she finally said. "We're getting married in a couple months, so he—um, *we*—thought it was a good time to come."

"Six weeks," Gabe said.

Lisa looked blankly at him.

"We're getting married in six weeks," Gabe said to Bruce.

Lisa's skin tingled with irritation so she drew in a long, deep breath, silently through her nose, and held it. When the feeling passed, her skin was covered in goose bumps and she felt jumpy, unsettled. She crossed the room and dropped onto the couch into the space left for her by Gabe's arm. She exhaled. Her muscles slackened and started to warm, sitting next to Gabe. Bruce stood frowning at them for a moment, and then he too sat, on the edge of the chair across from them. He kept his knees apart and rested his elbows on them. His hands dangled between his legs. The tremor was still there. He caught Lisa's eyes examining his hands, and barked out, "Lithium."

"Excuse me?"

"That's the goddamned shaking. The lithium."

Lisa nodded, looking at the carpet. The room went silent.

"You need money?" Bruce asked after a while.

"What?" Lisa said.

"Money? For the wedding?"

"No sir, we certainly don't," Gabe said quickly. "But thanks."

"For what? I wasn't offering any. Just trying to figure out why the devil you're here. Maybe to check out the old man? Make sure he's—"

Sarah hurried back into the living room and perched on the arm of Bruce's chair, closing both hands on his shoulders.

"Bruce, your daughter wanted to meet you, like we've already discussed," she said, her voice soothing, smooth as satin.

"Ever the social worker," Bruce snorted. Sarah colored. Bruce continued, "Did she tell you that's what she does? All day long, social work, fixing people's lives. That's how it is, the fixers and—fix*ees*." He laughed a gruff laugh. "She fixes, fixes, fixes at work, then comes home and tries to fix *me*." He laughed again.

"Well, it's worked pretty well for fifteen years!" Sarah said.

Lisa cleared her throat. She felt as if she were watching a movie starring an actor she had heard of but never before seen.

"You—you've been married fifteen years?" she said. I was eight then, she calculated.

"Yes, next month," Sarah said. "And don't you let Bruce's manner put you off. This grumpiness keeps people away, but it's really just his way of protecting himself. He's a softie on the inside."

Bruce snorted and shrugged his wife's arm off his shoulders.

"God's sake," he said. "See? There she goes, counselor mode."

A kettle screeched in the other room, and Sarah sprang up and disappeared. Lisa's eyes flitted all around the room, trying to read the titles on the spines of the books surrounding them, taking in the faded prints on the walls, and finally coming to rest on a framed eight-by-ten photo of Bruce, Sarah, and two young girls.

"You doing all right?" Bruce said, so abruptly that Lisa jumped. She turned to find Bruce's narrowed eyes on her, but his eyebrows were angled slightly up, deepening the creases in his forehead, as if that was his customary expression. Gabe patted her thigh. How warm and solid he felt beside her, like a massive oak or an immovable outcropping of rock!

"I've been doing pretty good," she said.

"She's in medical school," Gabe said.

Bruce's furry eyebrows inched up, and he nodded. His eyes slid across the sofa and came to rest on Gabe.

"Good for her. And you—you in medical school?"

"Me?"

"You."

Lisa's eyes were drawn back to the photo on the wall. The girls were dark-haired and looked about ten and twelve. She heard Gabe say, "I work the specialty cheese counter of our local organic grocer, Wellspring—"

"Cheese? You sell cheese? And you're how old?"

"Twenty-four."

"You're twenty-four and you sell cheese?"

"It pays the rent, and gives me time to do—"

"And *how* long have you two known each other?"

"Who are the girls in that picture?" Lisa cut in, turning back to them. She noticed Gabe's flushed face and Bruce's intense stare, and wanted to rise and place her body between those raptor's eyes and Gabe. But she only inched closer to Gabe, stroked his arm.

"Who are those girls?" Lisa repeated, hearing her voice brittle as ice. At that moment Sarah returned, carrying a teak tray with four steaming mugs on it.

"Those're our daughters, Ashley and Eleanor," Sarah answered for Bruce. "Maybe next time you can meet them, Lisa, but today I thought it would be best if it was just your father and you and—"

"She's gonna marry a twenty-four-year-old clerk in a grocery store," Bruce muttered to Sarah.

Lisa shot to her feet.

"I think that's our cue to go," she said, cheeks burning.

"Leese," Gabe said.

"Just for your information, though, he's not a *clerk* but the cheese *buyer* for one of the most upscale organic grocers in the entire Southeast, not that it would matter one bit to me if he *were* a clerk, and furthermore who the hell are you to—"

"Leese," Gabe whispered, tugging on her arm. At the same time she saw the corners of Bruce's mouth curl upward in a smile, and a rage began to whirl in her head like a cyclone, making everything around her go white.

"No—let me finish! You—a—*stranger*—with no effect on my life, somehow feel you have the right to pass judgment on the man I've chosen? The decisions I make have absolutely nothing— *nothing*—to do with you." The angrier she felt, the softer her voice got, until she could only squeeze out a hoarse whisper.

Bruce pinned her with his dark eyes.

"I'm trying to figure out what you two have in common. Whether you're equals. Whether he'll make you happy," Bruce said. "You been hospitalized yet?"

Now Lisa felt her knees fold under her, and she sank back next to Gabe.

"No," she said weakly.

"Good. See? By your age, I'd already had my psychotic break. Good." The creases in his forehead softened.

"Bruce—" Sarah cut in.

"She should know these things. *He*—" Bruce motioned with his tea cup toward Gabe, "he should definitely know these things. I don't know how much her mother told her. But here she is, so she must want information. Facts. *Him*, too."

"Facts aren't everything," Sarah mumbled, but Bruce went on as if he hadn't heard.

"You know she's got insanity in her genes, my side of the family?" he said to Gabe.

"Lisa's told me everything, sir."

"I believe in complete hones—" Lisa began, but the word evaporated from her lips just as Bruce's eyes widened slightly in surprise. Bruce's eyes narrowed again, and he looked her up and down. Without warning she felt a burning in her nose, and bit her upper lip until it went numb.

"Your mother tell you how I used to parade up and down Pennsylvania Avenue, back when we lived in D.C., stark naked? How I thought I was the son of Elvis, and would show up at recording studios demanding they cut my next record? How my mother had me committed three times? No? Shelly didn't tell you all that, did she, Lisa?"

"Didn't stop you from having two other kids," Lisa spat, and to her horror she felt tears stinging her eyes. She looked at the floor and tried to recall names of anaerobic bacteria.

"Those are Sarah's daughters," Bruce said, and his voice softened. "Those girls aren't stuck with an iota of my DNA. They're lovely girls. Eleanor just started college. I adopted them because they needed a daddy."

"Bruce is making it all sound much worse than it really is, his manic-depressive problem," Sarah said brightly. "We all have strengths and weaknesses. There's no guarantee Lisa inherited what you have. And besides, you've been so well on the medicine." She turned toward Lisa and Gabe. "Not a single hospitalization the entire time we've been together. Really. So don't you believe it's as bleak as all that."

"Devil's bargain. Gave up the pottery, the painting, the university professorship. Teach high school art," Bruce mumbled. He frowned into his tea.

"But—that's really cool, sir," Gabe said. Bruce said nothing, but tilted his frown up toward Gabe. Lisa's stomach spasmed with irritation, and then a wave of guilt as she realized the irritation was again directed at Gabe, not Bruce. She pictured the three-foot-tall ceramic urn which her mother used as an umbrella stand, which Bruce had made twenty-five years before. As a little girl, she'd stare at the fiery red and gold swirls that ran across its surface, and run her fingers across the ceramic cherubs that stood out in relief. It was beautiful. She wished she could make something like it. She'd imagine disappearing into the urn—had once tried to fit inside it after an argument with her mother, but it was too narrow.

"So, back to you. How long have you known him? What do you see in him?" Bruce asked Lisa, again fastening his eyes onto hers. A wave of fatigue washed over her, and her stomach tightened.

Gabe twisted to face her. He too seemed interested in her answer. She tried to swallow the lump in her throat. She heard herself say, "We've known each other a few months only, but—talk about love at first sight! I mean, he's the sweetest, most thoughtful guy. He anticipates my every need and—"

"What do you do, besides sell cheese?" Bruce shot at Gabe.

"Well, I—I play ultimate Frisbee, and I'm trying to get in a band, and—"

"Graduate from college?"

"Well—yes, sir, of course—"

"And you." To Lisa. "You play Frisbee? You into rock?"

Lisa slapped the couch.

"What is this, the third degree? This visit is not about Gabe's qualification to be my husband. Leave him out of your interrogation. What do I see in him? He—he's a great guy. His every thought revolves around how to best take care of me. No one's done that before. O.K.? That's enough. None of this has anything to do with you."

"You sure about that?" Bruce asked.

The white rage burning in Lisa's head brought words from her lips without a moment's hesitation.

"Yes, I'm *sure*. You know nothing about me, what I might need or not need, and that's been exactly what you wanted so you should be happy." A violent trembling started in her chest as the thoughts of all Bruce didn't know flooded her brain. How in high school she'd avoided bringing friends to the cluttered apartment Shelly rarely cleaned because she was too busy working two jobs. How her mother's mouth used to tighten when Lisa pointed out that her pants *again* skimmed an inch above her ankle bone, and they needed to go shopping. "Gabe, I think it's *really* time to go," she said.

"You're the one wanted to come here," Bruce grumbled.

"I'm *not* the one who wanted to come."

"Really? So he says 'jump' and you say, 'how high?'"

Lisa was on her feet, face turned toward Gabe, tugging on his sleeve. She was trying to pull a boulder. Gabe mouthed something at her. She flushed, and shrugged as if she didn't understand. Gabe rose at last, leaned toward her. His breath was warm and damp against her earlobe. She shivered. She shook her head once at Gabe, widening her eyes in an attempt to send a panicked message to Gabe's eyes beneath the radar of Bruce's gaze. Of course Bruce noticed. He watched them both with a frown, squinting.

In her ear, Gabe whispered again, "Ask him. We came all this way. Invite him."

Two weeks ago they'd been at the dining table of their tiny apartment, addressing the creamy wedding envelopes, when Gabe casually said, "I thought maybe we should invite your dad to the wedding." She recalled her sense of incredulity, the strangled silence. Gabe's calm voice saying, "Y'know, I'm not used to the messed-up-family deal. The way I see it, you and I should mend fences, get our stuff resolved before starting a family of our own. A clean slate. Plus—I thought if we get both your parents walking you down the aisle, it could be like—my wedding present to you."

And he'd smiled, that expectant, hopeful smile, and before she knew it she was agreeing to everything, to anything.

But now, in Bruce's living room, she stepped away from the red mouth, the soft lips. She stared at Gabe.

"You've *got* to be kidding," she whispered.

Sarah was on her feet now too, but Bruce remained seated, his lips curled in a smug smile.

"Lisa, believe it or not, Bruce is a loving father who wants so much for his children. He wanted so much for you—but—well, it's not always easy to see. He has tried to do what he thinks is best for you, in his own way—I mean, staying away, he thought that would help you, since he has such trouble seeing himself as someone who can have a positive influence—" Bruce grunted, but Sarah continued. "So please don't take—"

Now Gabe put up his hand, stopping Sarah.

"There's no need to apologize, really," he said, and his voice was even, mellow, too smooth. "Lisa and I are planning a beautiful wedding. Picture this." He framed the air with his hands. "It's gonna be on the beach, at sunset, really cool. Guitars strumming in the background. People barefoot in the sand. Lisa's totally excited

about it. She's very happy, Bruce, sir. She's not messed up or anything like that. She doesn't dwell on the past—she looks forward,
always forward. Nothing in the past matters to her. But she's getting
married in six weeks, and starting her own little family—well,
hopefully it won't be little for too long—and she came here because
she'd be—she wanted—that is, we'd *both* be—honored—if *both* her
mother *and* her father could be there, sir. You know—start us off on
the right foot. We're all one family now."

Everything in the room went still, miniaturized in the glassy
expression in Bruce's eye. Then Lisa felt the room bend and begin
to rotate and she glanced longingly at the couch, but Gabe's arm
around her waist held her propped up against his side. His hand
caressed her hip. She was the bride doll pinned to the top of a cake
and looked at Gabe, saw the smile on his lips as he waited for Bruce's
reply, and she tried to bend her own mouth into a smile to match
Gabe's and found she could do it, she could smile. The words *unified
front* flashed irrelevantly across her mind. She didn't want Bruce
at her wedding because he was everything that was bad in her life,
everything evil, and what had today proved but just that? She felt
vindicated in wanting to leave him far behind. She wanted Bruce to
have nothing at all to do with her adult life, her life as a competent,
mentally healthy wife and doctor. But if Gabe wanted Bruce at their
wedding, if he thought it would fix things . . . fix *her* . . . well, she'd
just grin and bear it and get on with things after. It was just a day,
after all. Just a drop in the bucket.

She tried to block out everything but the touch of Gabe's fingers
against her jeans. In the same slow, gentle way, his fingers sometimes
caressed her throat, her shoulder, her breast. Sometimes they mas-
saged her temples as she read late into the night.

She heard her name spoken, muffled as if through sleep. She realized her eyes had been glued to the coffee table. She lifted them and scanned the room. Everyone was silent and everyone was looking at her. She put her hand up to smooth her hair, and looked at Bruce.

"I said, do you want me at your wedding?" Bruce said roughly. Images flashed through her brain like a slide show: Shelly baking a cake the morning of Lisa's sixth birthday, after working a double shift; kids on the playground asking if her father was dead. Shelly saying, "I'll make it up to you—I'll be both mother and father." The extra ticket at high school graduation; the empty chair at her college science award dinner. Her mother's eyes when Lisa told her, over an expensive lunch at Fearrington, "I have found a man who will always love me, Mom, so don't you worry about me any more."

Did she want Bruce at her wedding? She felt the burning stares of everyone in the room. She was so tired. How could she tell what she wanted, today? If Gabe thinks you should be there, she wanted to say, come. Instead she said, "If you want to come."

Gabe reached into the backpack she hadn't even noticed him carry into the house, and produced a cream-colored envelope. Sarah took it from his hand, with a sunny smile. Gabe smiled back at Sarah. Bruce ran his hand over his mouth, didn't take the envelope from Sarah, and instead continued to study Lisa, head cocked to one side.

"You really love this guy?" he asked. His voice had dropped in volume, speaking to her as if no one else was in the room. Something in her chest released. Gabe's fingers tightened their grip on her hip, and she heard him say, "I'm going to take really excellent care of her, sir," and Lisa knew he would.

"What I'm asking is, do you really know him enough to love him?" Bruce said to Lisa, as if Gabe hadn't said a word. "Do you know yourself? People go through their lives blind as bats. Thumping into walls, pretending it doesn't matter. I know a thing or two about the world, and how things can turn out, if you're not careful . . ." Careful, Lisa heard. Her heart clenched, cooled. Her voice rose.

"Of course I love him," she answered, and she believed it. At the same time her throat constricted as she caught something in the way Bruce's forehead furrowed, in the way the light vanished from his eyes, that she would remember years later, after the short walk down the make-shift beach aisle lined with flaming torches, escorted by Gabe's father because Bruce did not come after all.

Bruce's expression was nothing in that moment if not sad, aching with sorrow, and Lisa would wake up one morning eight years later, after a busy night on call in her rheumatology practice, and hear Gabe humming to himself as he cooked her breakfast (eggs and sausage which she'd told him she did not want but which he insisted were good for her energy post-call) and she'd hear the humming interrupted only when he rushed off to pick up their baby, who had awoken and was crying in his crib. Lisa would swing her legs over the side of their bed, pause on the edge, and think, when was the last time I paused to think about anything? Bruce's lost, hooded eyes would flash into her mind, accompanied by Sarah's words, *facts aren't everything*. Caught in the frenzy of days at the hospital, rushing from one place to the next, stomach already heavy with baby number two, as planned, Lisa would sit on the bed and think, what do Gabe and I really have in common?

The thought would knock the wind out of her. She'd rush into a steaming shower and let the hot water run down her face, trying to melt the thought and the slow, heavy rise of sorrow in her chest. She'd tell herself, you've got a husband who is devoted, reliable. A man who is everything your father was not, and nothing that he was. You've proven that Bruce doesn't matter, that you can be a success in spite of him. Everything's going according to the plan you and Gabe outlined when you first met.

And for the first time she would let herself wonder if that was enough.

American Dreaming

*P*ranee kneels before the toilet in Mrs. Allen's third bathroom, her small upper body gyrating as she pushes the yellow sponge all around the porcelain rim. Her lips move and now and then she shakes her head. That girl, that girl, she mutters aloud. When she hears a door open she goes silent. Listening to the click-click of heels on the terra cotta tiles in the kitchen, the thud of grocery bags against granite countertops, Pranee thinks, Mrs. Allen is a mother of daughters. Mrs. Allen would know what to do.

"Hi Pranee! How's it going?" her employer calls from the other room.

"Fii-ine!" Pranee stretches the word into a high-pitched, two-syllable song while she rifles through the bottles in her cleaning basket, pulls out the nearly-empty Windex, and springs to her feet.

The kitchen hums with the crinkling of paper bags. When Pranee thrusts the Windex bottle at Mrs. Allen and says, "Need more," she sees Mrs. Allen's spine straighten and reads surprise in her eyes. Normally Pranee leaves the empties on the counter and can expect new supplies the following week. Pranee squints up at Mrs. Allen, who is a head and a half taller than she and whose silvering hair is drawn back into a ponytail. As Mrs. Allen's gaze travels up and down Pranee's ninety-pound frame, Pranee tucks the edge of her neat blue rayon blouse back into her blue-and-white sarong, adjusts a bobby pin slipping from her short black hair.

"O.K.—I'll get more—Windex," Mrs. Allen says in a halting, uncertain voice.

"Emmy, she like college?" Pranee says, after a beat of silence. Her hands pick up where Mrs. Allen's left off, mechanically stacking cans of tomatoes, dropping large green apples into the fruit basket. Mrs. Allen starts to fold paper bags.

"Yes, she does."

"My May—that May, I don't know she even go to college," Pranee says. Two apples slip her grasp and thump to the floor. Pranee scowls and retrieves them. As she straightens she catches Mrs. Allen's quick check of the clock on the microwave.

Pranee has heard Mrs. Allen compare her to a sparrow. She knows her employers like her to be a silent flurry of rapid motion, but she takes a gulp of air and speeds up her words: "May, she seventeen. Senior year. Everyone say, 'Pretty, that girl.' Too pretty. All she care about, how her hair look, how her clothes look. College application, just sit on desk. No good. I'm scared." She looks directly into Mrs. Allen's eyes.

"What a thing to worry about!" Mrs. Allen's syllable of laughter sounds like a cough. "You're only young once. Didn't you have some fun, at seventeen?"

Pranee touches the raised patch of skin on her left forearm, sees her seventeen-year-old self moving the pot of noodles at the same moment as her father moved the charcoal grill in their street stall, recalls the searing sting of the burn. But it was midday and neither had time to stop; she wrapped a dishcloth around her arm and kept counting skewers of chicken into portions, kept slicing mango to sell with sticky rice. Her nostrils widen at the memory of the mingled scents of coconut milk and the peanut sauce her father added to his curries.

"I'm scared," Pranee repeats. "I say to her don't go with boys. They trouble. Boy start coming around, brother of her friend, he twenty-two. He done with college. May, she get college applications, show me pictures. She say, 'See Mom?' Then boy comes, one time, two, three, now four weeks boy is coming, May not do applications. What he want with May?"

"It's normal. Emmy had her first boyfriend when she was— what? Fifteen? Cute little guy named Louie Blackstone. Father works with Thomas over at Duke. We thought it was a hoot!" Mrs. Allen's mouth broadens into a smile, and she sighs. Then she clears her throat. "It helps when you know the family. Do you know the family of this boy, coming to see May?"

Pranee shakes her head. In her mind she ticks off the families she knows: The Schmidts on Mondays and Fridays, Dr. Tomlinson who's divorced on Tuesdays. The Allens Wednesdays. Cordosas alternating with Wus on Thursdays. Sometimes the Griffiths and the Allens again on Saturday or Sunday, if they're entertaining.

"What does your husband say about May dating?"

"Barry?" Pranee snorts. She pictures his lip curling with derision at her, his blue eyes already focused beyond her as they speak.

"Barry, he say 'Nooooh problem.' *Everything,* no problem with
Barry. I say to her, 'May-may, you stay home study,' Barry say, 'Here
are car keys.'" A sharp laugh erupts from her throat. She folds her
arms across her chest, hugging herself, suddenly chilled. Her bones
feel thin as forsythia shoots through the rayon. Her voice rises in
a sing-song imitation of her daughter. "May say, 'Mom, you don't
know American ways.'" Pranee shakes her head. "American ways,
Thai ways, I say men same ways all over."

Pranee knows it's the expression on her face that interrupts Mrs.
Allen's chuckle. She tries to master her facial muscles and smile, but
her lips quiver.

"Well, if you don't want May seeing this boy you should talk with
Barry and the two of you should say no, together. You know—
unified front."

Pranee nods and notices the restless way Mrs. Allen's index and
third fingers drum against her upper arm. The grocery bags are
folded and the floor is spotless. Pranee pinches a few stray crumbs
between thumb and forefinger and strokes the counter-top the way a
mother might brush stray hair out of her child's eyes.

"Sometimes I think, I go back to Thailand. Try Bangkok. Too
hard here. Daughters—too hard. Sons easier. My Lin, good boy, no
problem. I go back, Barry raise May."

Now Mrs. Allen's eyes widen in alarm, and her forehead creases
with concern.

"Oh—no—no! You can't go away! What would I do without
you?"

"You call 'Merry Maid.'" Pranee's voice is shriller than she
intended. She turns abruptly to hide the pinched set of her lips and

retraces her steps toward the bathroom. "Look in yellow pages, big ad, 'Merry Maid.'" Mrs. Allen's heels click behind her, pausing on the marble threshold.

"It can't be better for you in Thailand!" she says, her voice soft. "And my goodness, what would May and Barry do without you?"

"My village, my mother is Muslim, my father was Muslim. We cover our arms. Here, May, she run around skinny skinny straps, no sleeves on her shirt. I say, 'Come pray with me.' She say, 'No, Mom! I'm not Muslim, that your thing!'"

Her high-pitched, trilling laugh spills out but her nose stings as it used to when she used to cry. At least they're talking about May again.

"Pranee, it's just adolescence. Emmy was like that too. May'll grow out of it."

"In Thailand, no adolescence."

"Well, May is American. It'll be fine."

Pranee slips her slim hands into oversized yellow rubber gloves. She rubs the sink silently, lips pressed together. All she can think to say is, "I'm so scared," but she's already said that so she says nothing. She thought Mrs. Allen would have more concrete advice, but perhaps she hasn't asked the questions well enough, clearly enough. Perhaps Mrs. Allen is about to say something now. Pranee lifts her eyes to the mirror and sees Mrs. Allen's eyes scanning the toilet, the mirror, the sink. Then Mrs. Allen, meeting Pranee's reflection, smiles.

"You really do such an amazing job, Pranee. We're so lucky to have you."

May's long, lean torso sways with each stroke of the brush through her elbow-length hair. She's bringing out the natural reddish tint in her black hair—the envy of her friends. She tries to ignore the reflection of Pranee pacing back and forth, back and forth in her bare feet just outside the bathroom. She wishes she could close the door, but Pranee would just rap on it and ask what she's doing. How she'll ever get any privacy in a two-bedroom with paper-thin walls, May doesn't know.

"It's just music, Mom!" May finally says, her face red.

"Don't shout your mother."

"Jeez! I'm not shouting—"

"American boys, they want one thing!"

"Mom, I'm an American girl, you know! Maybe *I* want the same thing!"

Pranee's pacing stops and she stares at May in the mirror, black eyes wide. May looks away first and sighs. She lays the brush beside the sink and picks up eye-liner, then focuses on herself, encircling her almond-shaped eyes with kohl. Pranee, whose reflection is dwarfed by hers, blurs.

"We're just going to hear music. His band is playing. I want to hear them."

"Where this?"

"I don't know exactly. Someone's house, Hillsborough."

"Music at a house? I know what kind music *that* is!"

"You don't know," says May, then clamps her lips together to keep the word "anything" from slipping out. She sighs. "It's called a house concert. People have them around here. They're in the papers, which you'd know if you knew how to—" another clipped word. Her cheeks color unevenly. She steals a glance at her mother, but Pranee has turned her back to May, has moved toward the windows.

"Look at rain. Gonna flood tonight."

May applies lip gloss with her finger, presses her lips together, puckers then relaxes them. Joining Pranee at the window, she shrugs at the sheets of water washing over the glass.

"You're so negative. Derek's got four-wheel drive."

They watch trails of shimmering red: the brake lights of a Jeep.

"Hey—that's him!" May curls her toes into the carpet, tenses her muscles, to resist the urge to jump up and down. The Jeep slides into a parking space and barks out a staccato *beep beep!*

"He not come up?"

"We're in a hurry!" A bubble of excitement, of endless possibility, expands beneath May's sternum. She runs back to the bathroom, spritzes J.Lo Glow into the air, then closes her eyes and walks through the mist just as she's seen her friend Tammy do. In the mirror she practices the sultry look she saw in *CosmoGirl*: eyes half-closed, lips parted. Her face goes blank when Pranee materializes behind her, holding out a sweater. May reluctantly pulls it on, but she waves away the umbrella and rain jacket.

"Gotta go!" she sings, and she is gone.

When she was little May would disappear under her quilt, head and all, and lie without moving for as long as she could stand it, trying to not hear her parents. It was always the same argument: Pranee's high pitched voice and broken English, "When we buy own house like other people?" and Barry's low, then louder refrain, "All you care about is money. You knew I was still in school when we met—you knew full well. You want a house, no one's stopping you from working."

"What job I get, no school, no read?"

That was usually met with silence.

"I work work work clean houses 'til I die, and die poor!"

Under the quilt, May's body would warm, relax. She'd feel embraced and almost sleepy. Then without warning it would be too much. Her thick breath would be too moist to re-breathe, and, sticky with sweat, she'd claw the quilt away from her head and gasp the cool air of her room as it washed over her damp scalp. She'd shed her bed, and then her clothes, and rummage through her closet naked until goosebumps covered her arms and legs. Sometimes, she'd linger at the colorful sarongs her mother gave her which she never wore. She'd picture herself in tropical gardens where the lush flowers matched the bright patterns of the cloth. Then, shivering, she'd yank her fleece robe off its hanger and shut the closet.

Leaving the apartment, running through the driving rain into Derek's jeep while Pranee's eyes burn into her back, May feels just like she used to feel emerging from the blankets. Even though the heat is going full blast to defrost the windows and the car is stuffy, May gulps the air as if it is cool and dry. She presses herself into the leather upholstery of the molded seat and slides the seatbelt across her chest, but Derek stops her hand and says, "How about a hello?"

His own seatbelt is off. He smells of mints and cigarettes and something musky, spicy, as he leans toward her and brushes her lips with his. A spark of static electricity makes May jump, then giggle.

"Hello," May says, and involuntarily glances around the car. It is empty except for them. She buckles her seatbelt and says, "Tammy isn't coming?"

Every other time she's seen Derek, his sister has been with them.

"She's getting her own ride. I figured—I mean, it's been four weeks since we met and we haven't had a moment to ourselves—it's like high school!"

May nods and tries to put on the sultry look she practiced, but her face is hot and feels twitchy, like she's scowling, without the mirror. Derek's attention has already turned to the road, and he guns the engine, burning a little rubber as he peels out of the parking lot. May giggles again and then twists in her seat, glancing up toward the windows of her apartment. But the car turns and swings her line of vision sideways before she can tell if Pranee saw.

Pranee notices the chill in the apartment and checks the thermostat, sliding it back up. She suspects Barry slides it down to save on electricity. In May's empty room, she lifts the balled-up quilt from the bed, shakes it in mid-air and neatly drapes it back over the smoothed-out sheets. She folds the red tee May sleeps in and lays it gently on the pillow. By now May must be in Hillsborough. She wonders if May navigates for Derek the way she always has for her, then remembers that of course this boy has no problem reading maps, street signs, directions he himself has scribbled down.

The quilt on May's bed is expensive, with hand-appliquéd lavender and pink butterflies stitched onto a pale green floral pattern. Barry's sister in Connecticut sent it for Christmas the year May turned ten. At least Barry's family has been good to May, remembering her on birthdays and at Christmas. Pranee can't hate them as she did when Barry first told her, all those years ago, eyes gleaming, how his family was disowning him for marrying a Thai girl. She should have been more suspicious of his excitement, then. She understands now that his family must have sent the money that allowed Pranee,

Lin, May and Barry to get by the first year after May's birth, when Pranee couldn't work and Barry never brought home the full earnings of his night-time security guard job. She no longer can figure out whether it's Barry's family that has maintained the distance over the years, or Barry.

But at least they've met May, at least Barry took her up to Connecticut to visit, the year before his sister sent the quilt. If *they* can fold May into their family, Pranee thinks, perhaps someone like Derek could do the same. Perhaps May is every bit as American as she thinks. After all, she played with the girls Pranee nannied for years ago with no self-consciousness, and they with her. She learned to read and write just as easily as they did, while Pranee's job slipped away from her as the girls, aging, piled books in her lap and complained when she made up stories about the pictures rather than reading the words. "*That's* not how it goes!" they'd chorus. On Pranee's dresser is a photo of those blonde-headed twins. Their mother, Madeleine, a scientist at Glaxo and divorced, raised those girls on her own. It was Madeleine who told her any child in North Carolina could get a college degree, a good job, a house eventually. Pranee remembers it in that order. Start saving now, Madeleine said. Pranee repeats it to May.

Instead May spends her babysitting money on J.Lo Glow and lacy underwear. May never learned to save like Pranee's son Lin did. Even at fifteen, Lin put aside his tips from scooping at Ben and Jerry's. And yet, Pranee is sure she didn't just imagine the brightness in May's eyes when the glossy college brochures first bulged in their mailbox. Before this Derek started calling night after night.

"That girl," Pranee says aloud. She snorts and shakes her head recalling how she rewarded May's good grades with trips to the mall. If she'd said no to the stretch jeans that ride low on May's slim hips, or to the lacy push-up bra May pleaded for in Victoria's Secret . . . May at seventeen has Barry's family's full breasts, a white girl's reddish tint to her hair. A white girl's careless pout. Yet she's on the quiet side, dark-skinned, black-eyed, an exotic bloom. Pranee fears for what Derek wants from May, for what he himself may not even yet know he wants.

There are no streetlights along Route 70 into Hillsborough, and few headlights cross theirs. May is in a spaceship, the lights of the dash blinking like controls, high beams slicing through rain and darkness. A few bungalows fly past the window, then a clump of trailers. Then nothing. Farmland. Here and there pairs of glowing red circles flash in the gloom, and May makes out the outline of a cow, a horse. She waits for Derek to ask her something, to tell her something, but he slides a CD into the stereo and guitar music drowns out the possibility of talk. She begins to think he's forgotten that she's sitting beside him when his hand slides to her thigh, so casually it seems an accident. She wonders if he thinks he's resting against the upholstery when she feels his fingers caress the inside of her leg through her jeans. Her heart hammers irregularly.

She hears Pranee's voice, Pranee saying, "In Thailand, men buy girls, twelve, thirteen, fourteen, for own pleasure." May has heard this from the time she started middle school. "Use them up, throw them away. Girls, they nothing."

"We live in America," she tells herself, as she usually says aloud when Pranee starts. She takes a long breath through her nose and tries to empty her thoughts, but Pranee's voice is like a recording.

May studies Derek's profile in the dim light of the car. His nose is long and straight, and his chin square. He *is* cute. But how had she overlooked that clenching of the muscles in his jaw, the thin lips? She recalls Pranee's question, "What he want with *you*? Finish all the college girls?" Derek's hand on her thigh burns through the denim and her skin feels numb beneath it. In her head Pranee says, *Music at a house? I know what kind music that is!* May rotates her wrist back and forth, trying to catch light on the face of her watch but it's no use; all she knows is they've been driving for a long time. She no longer recognizes any landmarks, which says a lot. She knows Hillsborough like the back of her hand, from navigating to Pranee's clients' houses.

"How far is this place?" May asks, running her tongue over her lips. "Seems like we'd be past Hillsborough by now."

"We're almost there. You like the music?"

"Will there be other people there?"

Derek turns his head, and she sees the frown on his brow. His hand moves from her thigh back to the steering wheel where it looks like a fist. She swallows. Even seated she feels the difference in their height, notices the broadness of his shoulders. Swam varsity in high school, Tammy told May. She's looking straight out but can feel him glance at her again, then turn away. He says, "You know, you're—oh—shit!" and he abruptly swings the car to the left. They bump off the main road onto a muddy, rutted path embraced on both sides by trees. His knuckles are pale against the steering wheel and May wants to ask what she's said wrong. But when he pumps the brakes and shifts the car into park May pulls her sweater back over her spaghetti-strapped tank. She sees his frown at her gesture, and she swallows and holds her breath, looking out the front of the car, try-ing to be invisible. Low-hanging branches tap against the roof of the car. There is no other car, no house, no sign of life, in sight. Derek punches off the CD that had been playing and a gaping silence swal-lows the air around them. He turns to May, his jaw squared in the amber light of the dashboard.

"Are you—is something going on? Are you freaked out or some-thing about this?"

"About what?" she says. Her voice is raspy and trembles. She has never been alone in a room with Derek. He's been to college; he's had other girlfriends. *Girls, they nothing,* she hears Pranee say. She steals a glance at him.

"About what." He shakes his head, then, looking at her, scowls.

"Didn't I tell you it's in a barn? Off a dirt road? Don't you think I know what I'm doing? But look at you. You look terrified." He flips down the passenger sun visor, and in the faint circle of yellow light bouncing from and back into the mirror May sees her own wide eyes, the whites almost fluorescent. She blinks and shakes her head, but can't say a word. The girl in the mirror looks more Asian than May. She flips up the visor. When Derek cups her shoulder with his meaty palm she jumps. He withdraws his hand and slaps the dash.

"Man! You *are* afraid! I can't believe—oh, never mind." His voice seems amplified and May can't make a sound. Her mouth is dry and her stomach tight. Derek shakes his head again, his lips pulled down in disgust, and he shifts into drive.

May still can't talk. The car bounces and slips and she can't tell where they are.

Without warning the trees part and they bump across a wide, muddy field studded with cars. Hondas, pick-ups, BMWs angle haphazardly, parked facing all directions. Beyond the cars an elegant white clapboard house reigns on a small rise, smoke rising from the chimney, lights glowing in all the windows. Several smaller wood buildings surround the house. The knot of fear in May's stomach releases, leaving behind a dull, throbbing anger toward her mother.

"Well, this is it. There isn't enough time to take you home, you know. 'Cause I would. Maybe we should've brought Tammy with us."

May looks mutely at him, but he is looking straight ahead.

"I keep forgetting how young you are," Derek says, his voice softer now.

"I'm not young." May clears her throat, then squeezes her small icy palm around Derek's knuckles on the steering wheel, but he shakes his head and parks the car without looking at her.

"I don't know *what* the deal was back there, and I'm not sure I *want* to know," he says. "If you think I'm some frat boy who—some guy just looking for—oh, never mind." He turns to her. A muscle twitches in his clamped jaw. "I'm a musician, you know what I mean? And I'm going places, and it's gonna be fast."

May's head bobs up and down, chest full of dread. Perhaps she's missed the biggest opportunity of her life.

"Look, I—let's—let's just forget it, O.K.?" she says, running her tongue over her lips and trying to steady her voice. Her lip gloss feels congealed and sticky. When have Pranee's weird fears become hers? "That wasn't—me," she whispers.

"Didn't see anyone else in the car."

"Look—what was that music you were playing before? The CD. Was that you?"

Silence.

"Was that the band? *Your* band? C'mon." She leans across to his seat and tries to tickle him. Unsmiling, he pulls away.

"I mean, it was awesome. That CD. I hear you guys are awesome—that's what Tammy says. *Was* that you?"

He sighs, and then a smile sparks and fans out over his face.

"We are pretty damn good, aren't we?" His eyes return to her face and she tries to conjure up the models in *CosmoGirl,* in *Seventeen,* in *People* magazine. She tilts her head and juts her chin out and parts her lips and smiles at him, but he squints at her, a bemused look on his face. Then without warning he shrugs and jumps out of the car and she hears the slap of mud as his boots hit the ground. "All right—let's go," he calls, grabbing her hand, tenting his jacket over both their heads. They race across the field, the mud sucking at her shoes and the icy rain cutting into her eyes. Their destination seems to be a rectangular wooden barn, whose windows glow yellow. A neon sign blinks, "Open for Dancing." Derek props the door for May.

She is unprepared for the rush of happiness that sweeps over her when she steps into the room. The air is dry and warm, and guitar chords vibrate into her chest. The building contains this single unadorned, wood-paneled room lined with mismatched metal folding chairs. Nearly every chair is full. It's like a church, but instead of an altar, at the far end of the room two women with long silky hair and middle-aged faces sit on bar stools cradling guitars. Their harmonizing voices rise and fall, honey-smooth, beautiful.

Pranee looks at her wrist-watch. May has been gone over an hour. Is she surrounded by music and teenagers, or is the boy with that reddish-blond hair peeling off May's sweater, inching her thin straps over her shoulders? Pranee saw his bulky muscles through the thin fabric of his rugby shirt last time. He could pin May to her seat with one hand.

But he doesn't have to pin her. Did Lin's father have to do anything more than talk nicely to Pranee? Eat her curry, ball sticky rice between his thumb and forefinger and pierce her eyes with his and Pranee was ready to pour him free drinks, serve him extra mango. Spend the evening with him at the beach. When she told him she was pregnant his grimace pulled flat the skin of his neck and he couldn't spit the words out fast enough: of course it couldn't be his, he'd been careful, he had to return to Bangkok in a week to begin medical school, did she need money?

By the time she met Barry she'd learned. She talked less, smiled less. Barry at twenty was quiet himself. When he explained his year off from college to "find himself," she giggled at the phrase. Barry became talkative then, brought her small gifts, invited her to see America with him. When she declined, he was willing to tickle Lin under the chin and make funny faces until her little boy laughed; willing, finally, to take Lin along, willing to offer a ring.

As Pranee neatly aligns the college brochures on May's newly dusted desk, she hears May say, "You're lucky, Mom, you got out. You got to live here." Barry has May convinced that Pranee's family's street stall was abject poverty. He leaves out the solid feel of their cart, the clean bamboo steamers for the sticky rice, the charcoal grill twice as big as the stall's across the street. Pranee never went hungry. Her parents never threw her out on the street, even after her stomach started to swell and she could no longer stir the curries without feeling queasy. She doesn't tell May this. Instead each time they argue she says, "Yeah, I lucky. I meet your daddy—rich American, study Thailand, serious serious, a student." She should not say it, not to May, but she can keep it in no more than she can curb her staccato laugh. "Rich American, your father! My Lin, he send check every month or what would I do? That Lin, good boy."

The audience is entranced. Derek leads May toward the front of the room, where from the blur of unfamiliar faces spring the faces of her friends, including Tammy. His usual ease regained, Derek takes the only open chair and pulls May onto his lap. Strangers nod and smile at her as if they know her. She smiles back. Where had her brain been, in the car? She lives in North Carolina, not Thailand. If only her mother didn't always focus on the ways May is different from her friends. She's not. She's just like them.

Now her head is full of music and she feels its pulse in her veins. Derek has both arms wrapped around her, and he bounces her as he taps his foot in rhythm with the beat. The heel of his right hand has come to rest against her left breast, but she's sure it's sheer coincidence—he takes no notice. She tries to ignore that her left breast feels hotter than her right, and that her breath is coming very fast. She is part of this knot of happy people. She tries to focus on each lyric but the words swim in her mind. They rearrange themselves into Pranee's "How much money they make?" May shakes her head. She feels Derek's fingers stroking her hair and his breath warming the side of her neck.

He tugs gently on her hair and she looks at him.

"I'm up next," he whispers, just before the room bursts into thunderous applause.

Two hours since May left. Three.

Pranee wipes the last ochre drops off the counter top, and puts a cover on the curry she's just removed from the stove. "Dinner tomorrow, dinner next night," she whispers. She wipes her hands on a dishtowel, then grabs her special Thai broom—Mrs. Allen raves about it, made her drive to Burlington to find one like it—and drives it under every counter edge in the kitchen. Her knuckles turn white around the wooden handle. Barry told her to stay out of the bedroom a few hours while he works on his dissertation. He's almost there: ABD, all but dissertation. He's been ABD for years. She no longer argues with him about finishing, even though she now knows none of his classmates took more than a decade to finish *their* degrees. She pauses at the door to their bedroom, fingers the knob. Does he think she's deaf, that she can't hear his yells whenever the Blue Devils score? She knows it's basketball season.

Her hand abandons the doorknob. What would Barry say, anyway? *Let May be.* Pranee can never seem to find the words to say, *Have you felt the doors that slam in your face if you have no education? Do you want that for May?*

"That girl, that girl," she mutters into the stillness of her spotless kitchen.

Derek plays guitar standing up, hips jutting forward against his instrument, thrusting to the beat. His bangs shake as he moves to the music. He winks at the musician to his right, who plays an electric violin. Then he looks up from his guitar and his brown eyes lock onto May's. He smiles, winks at her, then sings every word directly to her, breaking their connection only to watch the fingers of his left hand as they skip over the frets during particularly complex melodies. People in the rows in front of May crane their necks to follow his gaze. Without warning, May finds herself smiling and strangers smile back.

Afterward she is carried on a tide of people to the big house on the hill. In a kitchen as large as her entire apartment, she has cheese and crackers and drinks wine from a plastic cup. Everyone wants to meet her. Derek finally pulls her by the hand into the silence of what looks like a home office. By the dim light of a single desk lamp, Derek kisses her long and steadily and she kisses back. She lets his fingers explore her narrow waist, her straight hips, then glide upward. She shivers when he cups her breasts, then smiles when his fingers run through her hair. He kisses her again so forcefully that his teeth click hers and she tastes blood. She draws away, her hand still grasping his shoulder. She is amazed by the change in his eyes: half-shut, pupils dilated, hungry. His breath comes quickly and in ragged jabs. She kisses his cheek and he closes his mouth and pulls away from her, tucks his shirt back into his jeans.

"Do you sing?" he asks in a thick voice.

"What?"

"Do you sing?"

She laughs and swings her hair. Her head feels like it might float away.

"I like to. But not like those women in there—"

"It doesn't matter. Our stuff's too loud and fast for people to hear

American Dreaming

....

42

you like they hear them. But—y'know, we could use a girl—someone as gorgeous as you—you see how everyone just loved you tonight! You'd look awesome up there, dancing, with that hair and your—*look*—we could give you a tambourine to hit or something."

His eyes are beginning to return to normal, but her blood is pounding in her ears.

"Really? Me—in the band?"

"I'll ask the guys."

"That would be so cool!"

"You could take a year off—tour with us even."

There are so many things she can do, so many people she can meet. Even this house—who knew there are people who live in such mansions and have barns built just to hold *concerts*? May thinks of her parents' cramped apartment, the restricted circle of her mother's trips, day in, day out, the Cordosas, the Allens, the Griffiths. She moves closer to Derek, allows him to guide her hand toward his crotch, hears his soft moan.

Pranee is pacing the living room when the door inches open. She has changed out of her work clothes into a good blue-green sarong and a thin white cotton sweater.

"Don't you ever sleep?" May says, frowning. Pranee smiles while her eyes inspect May head to toes.

"Dad asleep?"

"You don't *hear*? Snore like bear. No trouble eat, no trouble sleep . . . just trouble *work*." Pranee laughs. "Boy kiss you?"

"What?"

"College boy. He try use you up?"

"*Mom*! Please don't talk that way about Derek. You don't know him. The music was—like—*professional*. And guess what?" May's face becomes animated. Her words spill faster. "He wrote a song for me. He told the whole audience the song was for *me*, and he—"

"He not kiss you?"

May closes her eyes and pulls air in sharply through her nose. Her cheeks are flushed and her forehead looks damp.

"That is none of your business."

"Ah! *Of course* he kiss you!" Pranee springs between May and the doorway to May's room. "What else twenty-two-year-old want with seventeen-year-old? Ha!"

"How can I even talk to you? It's like talking to a—thirteen-year-old!"

Pranee stiffens.

"You right, I not so smart like you. You—you so smart you not need college?"

"College again? God, Mom, I don't know. I don't know *what* I should do next year," May says in a near whisper. Pranee wants to grab her shoulders and shake her, slap her cheek. Embrace her.

"You don't know? You good student, A's and B's, read so good I proud, you smart girl and you *don't know*?"

Pranee makes a low throaty sound. May presses both palms against the sides of her head.

"Mom," she says. "Just listen a moment. *Anyone* can go to college—that's what Derek says. The people I met tonight built themselves a building just to have a place to play music. Can you imagine that? *For fun.*"

There's so much Pranee wants to say. She wants to tell May that it might seem like she can do the same things as the kids whose parents are rich, but in the end, those with money end up in a different place than those without. She wants to explain how she thought she was choosing well when she chose Barry, choosing an educated man, but how much better off she'd have been getting an education herself. Once the second baby—May—came, there was no chance for Pranee to do anything for herself. She wants to remind May how Madeleine, the scientist at Glaxo, was fine even when her husband left her—because she had a career, an education. What she says is, "Girls they have fun young, then fun gone—gone when old! Boys different."

May kicks her feet out of her platform shoes so abruptly that they drop with a crash, narrowly missing Pranee's bare toes.

"Don't tell me again about how girls get used up in Thailand. You know what that does to me? Tonight, I even started worrying with Derek, even though I *know* him so well. God, I felt like such an idiot . . . the coolest night of my life, and I almost ruined it by being scared."

"Scared, that's good," Pranee says. She wants to take May into her arms, twist her long hair into a bun, run a washcloth over her cheeks and the back of her neck. Scrub the scent of cigarette smoke and foreign perfume, other people's soaps and shampoos, off her daughter.

"Mother, scared is *not* good." The scenes May described evaporate, leaving the two of them back in the cramped kitchen beside the burn mark on the linoleum counter. May wrinkles her nose and says, "*Curry.* I see tomorrow is a Taco Bell night for me."

"Write college application, then go Taco Bell."

"You never pushed Lin to go to college! Navy right out of high school was good enough for him!" May retraces her steps toward her room, Pranee at her elbow.

"Lin good boy," Pranee says, and for a moment she pauses. How can she explain there wasn't the same dangerous period for Lin? That Lin can go to college later?

"Yes, I know, he's perfect." May takes advantage of the yard that briefly gapes between them and slips into her room, noiselessly shutting the door. Pranee blinks, then stands frozen in front of May's closed door. Her life has become a string of closed doors. She rubs her arms, touches the pocket of her sweater. Her wristwatch reads 3:30. She waits another minute, two, five, then, without knocking, shoves open May's door.

The room is dark except for the small reading lamp next to May's bed. When Pranee bursts in May's arms fly across her body as if to shield nakedness. May is examining herself in her full-length mirror, dressed in the gold-and-red sarong Pranee gave her for her sixteenth birthday, the one she has never seen her touch. Pranee sucks in a breath. May has coiled her hair into a tight knot secured with a pencil, just the way she always refuses to wear it. It reveals her cheekbones, her slender neck. In the dim light May could pass for Asian.

Pranee flips on the ceiling light. May squints, blinks. Strips down to her underwear and Pranee sees with dismay the lacy bra they bought last month and matching lace underwear she doesn't recognize. May disappears into her closet, and through the door mumbles, "What do you want, anyway? I'm trying to get to bed."

Pranee feels her eyes moisten, but she blinks and swallows. She squats to where the sarong lies in a heap at her feet. Carefully she lifts it and folds it back along its ironed creases.

"You know why I happy have money from Lin?"

May emerges from the closet wearing her night shirt. She rolls her eyes.

"Who cares?"

Pranee's fingers, inside the pocket of her sweater, touch the edges of an envelope. "You guess. Guess how I spend."

"I don't know. Groceries? You're always complaining how much food costs."

Pranee shakes her head.

"Guess."

"This is so stupid. I don't know—how? You claimed not to have enough to get me a car of my own last year," May says.

"I have car, I drive you places. We not talking about car."

May retreats to her bed, slides in under the sheets, yawns what Pranee can tell is a fake yawn.

"All right. I give up, all right? *What* do you do with the money?"

Pranee presses her lips together and perches on the side of the bed. She hands a plain white envelope to May.

"You look see," she says.

May sits up. Her pupils are large and there's a smattering of color across both cheeks. She twists a strand of hair around her thumb like she used to as a kindergartner, then reaches into the envelope. She pauses, then extracts a bank statement. Pranee's blood hums inside her veins. She watches the confused frown on May's face, watches her unfold the sheet of paper.

"Twenty-three thousand!" she gasps. Pranee smiles.

"You have twenty-three thousand in this CD and you complain when I have to get a new pair of jeans?"

Pranee snatches the statement out of May's hand, carefully slipping it back into the envelope. Her fingers caress the envelope flap back into place.

"All money Lin send me, I put in bank. All money I make extra, after pay bills and food, that too. Like Miss Madeleine showed me, long ago. Everything, I put in there so can pay for school." She waits for her daughter to spring from the bed and throw her arms around her neck, or for her eyes to brighten and the lovely white-toothed smile to enliven her features. Instead, May sits in silence, eyes down, features flat. Finally, she mumbles, "I never asked you to do that, Mom—I mean, *you* could use it to—you could—does Dad know?"

Pranee steadies herself against May's dresser. You'd think a daughter would see how it is, day in, day out, see who works and works and earns and who sits and lies and complains. But May knows Barry only as a father: one who lets her do what she wants and buy what she wants, with Pranee's money.

"Does Dad know about this money?" May repeats.

Pranee hesitates, then slowly shakes her head, eyebrows arched. Her eyes look directly into May's. In Thailand she could live on this money for a long, long time. She'd have to leave tomorrow because if Barry discovers the money, he'll fume about the secrecy and immediately claim it as his own. If Barry discovers the money, there will be nothing for school for May and no freedom for Pranee.

"Mom, you can't *bribe* me to go to college, you know. It's a free country."

"Yes, free country," Pranee whispers. "Free country, I clean houses fourteen years. Still same apartment, same clothes, no extra end-of-month money."

May sits up, pulling her legs under her and hugging her pillow to her chest. She's looking at Pranee as if seeing her for the first time. Pranee can't sustain the stare, and slides her eyes to the poster of the Backstreet Boys, pinned just behind May and next to Britney Spears. Everyone on May's wall is young, half-clothed, wealthy.

May's head is abuzz with new information. Her breasts tingle with the memory of Derek's touch, and she wants to draw the quilt over her head and be alone and replay his face, his swaying hips, his songs in her mind. But like an after-image burned into her retina, she also sees the numbers dancing on the page of Pranee's bank statement. As if for the first time she notices the thready muscles in her mother's arms, the uneven strands of hair that poke into Pranee's eyes because she won't pay to have someone else cut it. Her mother looks jittery, pale, and is uncharacteristically quiet.

"Mom," May says, "why don't *you* go to school?"

Pranee turns back at her with a scowl.

"That stupid idea," she says, and May rolls her eyes. But the filaments of thought that have been forming in her mind stretch, pull together, and she continues, "No, really. Why *didn't* you ever learn to read and write English? I've never thought about it before, but couldn't you—couldn't you even now—I mean. . . ."

Her words evaporate. Pranee is frowning at her, but May can detect a look of pleading. She suddenly pictures her father watching TV and as if for the first time, she sees his stomach bulging over his belt buckle, hears the irritation as he yells at Pranee for the noise of the vacuum as she pushes it around his chair. May can't put into words her next question: Why has *Barry* never insisted Pranee go to school? Barry, whose thesis is on the health and well-being of indigenous people in third-world economies? Barry, who whispered in May's ear when he took her to visit his family in Connecticut, *See the rich swine, they want to keep this privilege to themselves and not lift a finger to help anyone who is different from them.* The thought makes her head swim. Her limbs are heavy and her eyes gritty with fatigue. Like the fog on the road that disappeared as they approached it, May's memories of the evening shimmer and vanish. Her mother has not answered her question and May does not repeat it.

"So?" Pranee says.

"So what?" May echoes.

"So, you tell your father?"

May notices Pranee watching her like a cheetah, every muscle tensed, ready to pounce or flee at any moment. There is fear but also a kind of hunger in her mother's eyes.

"Tell Dad what?" May asks.

"About the money. *The money.* You tell him?"

"About your money? Of course not!" May says.

Pranee lets out a sigh of relief and a big smile unfolds across her face.

"You promise me? We on same side?"

May shrugs. Pranee is so hard to figure out sometimes, but this half-childlike, half-frightened expression in her eyes scares May.

"Of course. I promise, Mom," May says softly.

Pranee reaches for May's hand and squeezes it. Her usual energy returns in a surge. She bounds from the room like a child, singing, "Night-night! Go sleep, go sleep now!" May is more awake than ever. And her entire body begins to feel the weight of a promise much larger than the one she understood she was making.

Practical

When he opens the door to his imported bride, the woman who used him and betrayed him and has given him no happiness but his Nina, Alex forgets his rehearsed iciness, his mother's suggestion to make her tell her business standing in the hall. Her gray eyes peering up at him through her long lashes are bright with hope, and her flushed cheeks give her the feverish excited look she'd had when they first met. She is a woman who needs him again. He swells with the certainty that he was right all along, chose well after all; and that the moment has finally come when others see it. He grabs the hand she extends, kissing first her right cheek, then her left.

He chose her when she said, "You suffer from diabetes," just like that, before she ever pricked his finger or clapped a stethoscope to his chest. The other two were prettier, as Alex would bitterly remember later, and one was only eighteen, possibly still a virgin. But Viorica was not unpleasant-looking nor, at twenty-four, really past her prime. She had finished a medical degree, so he would not have to support her forever. If her prominent cheekbones gave her a slightly gaunt, hungry look, her feathered short black hair softened the effect. She had a birthmark too large to be called a beauty mark just above her lip, but her cat-like eyes were that clear, startling gray. In the end he decided a beautiful wife would only cause trouble once he brought her to America, attracting American men who were richer or thinner than he. A beautiful wife might have her own plans; leave.

Better a wife capable of seeing in him, in the recent doughy feel of his arms and the growing bulge of his stomach, not the ubiquitous obesity of single men in America forced to dine nightly at fast-food stands, but a genuine illness, something she could tend to, cure. Better a wife who nodded when he said, "I am a man without illusions; a man with simple needs." A blood test two weeks later confirmed Viorica's diagnosis of Alex. They were married within the month.

It wasn't until half a year later that she first castigated him for failing to ask what she wanted for her own life. What *you* want? he'd repeat, blinking his pale protruding eyes. What could she possibly want that would be a mystery? He imagined she wanted what every Romanian woman young enough to hope wanted: a chance at a better life. Money. Nice things to wear. A comfortable apartment in the wealthiest country in the world; what *he'd* wanted when presented with his own opportunity to flee Bucharest. Hadn't he and Viorica been straddling a see-saw, he, airborne and she, rooted to the bottom? He used his very weight to elevate her: his new American passport, his job at the cell-phone manufacturing plant, his spacious, modern condo. He balanced her life with his. He didn't guess that his very bulk could ground him, while she, light as a sparrow, might soar, floating into the sky. Away from him.

But he's a practical man and has always been. Here he is, kissing her cheek seven years after that first meeting and nearly a year after she moved out. Her skin is smooth; baby-powder scented. She doesn't return the kiss but she squeezes his shoulder. "I must see you, face to face," she'd said on the phone. She was never a big kisser. The see-saw can still be leveled. Living alone can change a person, and he is ready to forgive. They inspect one another. Her hair skims her cheeks and ends just above her chin, exactly as it did when he first saw her. In other ways she's entirely different. In lieu of her penny-sized birthmark she has only a tiny dimple above her mouth now. Her eyes are lined in kohl and she wears pale pink lipstick and a choker made of tiny, delicate pearls. Her body has filled out: rounder breasts, fleshier hips. Only her eyes remain hungry.

"I'm glad you called," he says in Romanian in response to her English hello. He sucks in his stomach and gestures into the living room of the three-bedroom condo they used to share. "Come in." Too late he notices the stale air, the lingering odor of the stuffed cabbage his mother cooked that morning. Viorica used to throw open the windows to let the spring air in. Her eyes pan the room. "Come on in," he repeats. Her eyes narrow, focusing behind him where the slap of footsteps against the sun-faded wall-to-wall carpet signals the arrival of his mother. Alex twists his neck. His mother hasn't bothered to change out of her terrycloth house robe and dollar-store slippers. She is a heavy-set, short woman with an impassive, pancake face. She folds her arms across her drooping breasts and stares at Viorica. Alex frowns. The two women nod to each another. His mother says, "So. You're back."

Alex clucks his tongue. "I asked you to stay in your room," he mutters under his breath, but Viorica's gaze skims over his mother's head. "Where's Nina?" she asks.

"She's at a neighbor's," Alex's mother says. "We didn't want her confused, *again*."

The small dimple above Viorica's lip twitches and her ribcage deflates. But she squares her shoulders and turns to Alex. Her delicate fingers alight on his arm, cool and dry, and he recalls the first time she took his pulse—the very first time she touched him. He shivers. Her voice is low and urgent; the words in English.

"I thought you understood over the phone—I have hope of a talk, a special, important talk. . . ." She swallows.

"Whatever you have to say to him, you can say in front of me," his mother says in Romanian.

"Mama!" Alex's eyes bulge behind his thick glasses. "Please!"

"We'll go out," Viorica says in English, grabbing his elbow with her free hand. "Let's drive to Durham, stroll through the gardens. Talk in open air." Viorica, who grew up with the specter of bugged apartments and tapped telephone wires, has always saved important talks for the outdoors.

"All the way to Durham!" his mother complains. "You can walk just as well around the parking lot here!"

"Take a jacket, Alex, is breezy," Viorica says.

He grabs a windbreaker from its hook in the hall with a meaningful nod to his mother. *You see how she still looks after me,* he wants to say. After the phone call he told his mother, *She wants back, I'm sure of it,* but his mother snorted and called him a fool.

Viorica is still a nervous driver, following glances in her mirrors with quick checks over her shoulder. She shushes his attempts at conversation, even when his questions require a simple yes or no.

Did she finish her residency? Has she been feeling well? Viorica needs silence to concentrate. It was just like this when she studied at his kitchen table: equal intensity for driver license test or medical school equivalency exams. She'd press the heels of her hands into her temples and read for hours, marathons of reading, her face three inches from the page.

"Here we are," she says, steering into a shady parking spot. "Have you been walking here, Alex? Have you been exercising?"

"I haven't had time."

He's not been back to Duke Gardens since she left. The Gardens were her discovery, one of her many manic pilgrimages after she got her license. She'd drop him off in Research Triangle Park early, and sometimes be thirty minutes late picking him up in the evening. His stomach fluttered with anxiety—and hunger—as he waited in the violet dusk. "Sorry—I got lost on my way back from Asheboro," —or Greensboro, or High Point, or Fayetteville, she'd say. "What is there in Asheboro?" he'd ask, his voice keening to a whine, and the gleam in her eyes would extinguish. "What is there here in *Morrisville?*" she'd reply.

He didn't think he needed to spell it out for her. In Morrisville was the three-bedroom condo he owned, with a large swimming pool beside which she could lie all day if she wanted, and barbecue grills in a picnic area they could use at will. There were supermarkets with apples piled in pyramids regardless of the season, and meat so fresh it bled beneath its cellophane wrap. New movies came out every Friday. It was no Bucharest, that was true—you couldn't stroll down a wide boulevard and smell the citrusy lindens, nodding at acquaintances, or settle into a *cofetarie* for a pastry and a bracing cardamom-laced Turkish coffee. But you could buy the smallest camera or the largest television in the world. You could run the air conditioning so high you'd need a sweater on a scorching day. You could park your car—your own car—steps from wherever you needed to be.

Viorica loops her hand through his arm and his chest brims with the thumping of his heart. He's been too long without a woman, not counting the paid escorts from the back pages of the paper. He says, "Look how the roses are opening. How many gardeners they must employ!" The sky is cloudless, Carolina-blue, as they say in Chapel Hill. Viorica closes her eyes and inclines her face to the sun. She stands like this for more than ten seconds—Alex begins to count. His brow crinkles. As long as he's known her she's been a blur of motion—clearly she's changed. He lifts a tentative hand toward her cheek, wanting to stroke the curve of her jaw, her long neck, her throat. She sighs and opens her eyes, and his hand freezes in mid-air, then clumsily diverts to rubbing his own chin. She smiles, takes his arm, then paces them at a stroll, steering toward the small gazebo at the top of the formal gardens. Its cap of fragrant wisteria rains lavender petals on them.

She settles onto a wrought-iron bench. Across from them, a young woman flanked by toddlers unwraps triangular crustless sandwiches from wax paper. "I need to see you, face-to-face," she'd said. Or was it, "I need to see your face"? He swats at the wisteria, trying to pluck a sprig to present Viorica but the vine is out of reach. He lets his thick hand drop on the tiny nub of Viorica's knee. "It's been too long," he says.

"You've gained weight." She slides his hand from her knee, but then holds on to it. She turns it over, inspecting his palm, pushing her thumb into the skin. "With your risk factors, Alex, really. Your father was just a year or two older than you are now when he died. Are you taking your medicine? Are you checking your sugars?"

He grunts. "Do you ever see men as simply men and not patients?"

Pink seeps across her throat and she squeezes, then abruptly releases his hand. She examines her lap, her jaw muscles twitching. When she turns back to him her eyes are flat and he feels a pang of regret. She's wooing him in her own way and he has to give her time: he has to give her the chance to come back to him without losing face. When they were together she seemed to never hear his suggestions, yet then she'd do things like grow her hair long as he'd requested. She is a woman of action, not words. Maybe in her enormous rush to become a success she swept right past happiness, and now she's trying to find a way back.

Viorica was in a rush from the moment her feet hit American soil. She signed up to take her medical equivalency exam just four months after her arrival, despite Alex's suggestion that she wait a year. Her failure barely made her falter. She allowed herself three days in bed, eyes swollen, hair unwashed. Then she spent a week watching television, all day every day, ignoring Alex's suggestions that she get out, take a walk, buy some groceries. He tried to convince her there was no hurry: "I make plenty of money," he'd repeat. She shrugged sullenly but complied with Alex's eventual demand that she resume cooking dinner. She was a speedy but indifferent cook—there were lumps in the *mamaliga,* and her steak was rubbery. She couldn't even reheat a ready-made pizza without burning the crust. He was almost relieved when she got hired at the mall and he found himself eating frozen dinners once again. How she kept that job was a mystery: every visit to the coffee kiosk found her sitting at the counter poring over medical books instead of waiting on customers.

But she passed her equivalency exam the following autumn, and by the holidays their bedroom was littered with residency program applications. He'd come home to find her feverishly writing and then balling up essay drafts. He didn't complain because she understood her duties toward him. If he surprised her from behind, nibbling the nape of that long neck while she wrote, she sometimes jumped but she never reprimanded him. She'd abandon her work, wrap her arms around his shoulders and let him hike her shirt up over her head. She was energetic in bed, if a bit hurried there too. When it was over, when he lay huffing on his back, fumbling for a cigarette, she'd wrap herself in a sheet and return to her essays, not missing a beat even to shower.

Alex's body buzzes with desire at the memory of Viorica's arms lifted in the air, the rayon blouse slipping over her pale, firm breasts. She never wore a bra while studying at home. He leans toward her, inhaling her faint lavender fragrance along with the wisteria scent and parts his lips but before he can speak she says, "Let's talk about our Nina." There is a tremor in her voice. She squints as she looks into his face although the sun is behind her, slanting, if anywhere, into *his* eyes.

"*Nina?*" he says. His body reacts as if yanked from his warm downy bed onto the cold floor of morning. He clears his throat and adjusts his glasses, his face hot. "Nina. Nina is great."

"Tell me." She leans toward him, touching his hands. Her lips part and the tip of her tongue flicks over them for an instant. "Tell me everything."

He shakes his head to clear it and swabs his forehead with a tissue.

"Everything about Nina? Hmm. O.K. She—she can't wait to start kindergarten. I don't know what they can teach her because she already knows how to read." His body is cooling; his pulse is normal now. "English *and* Romanian. A bit of the Russian alphabet. Mama has been doing a great job with her."

Viorica nods. "You stopped sending pictures. I thought I'd see her today."

"Mama didn't think it was a good idea. For Nina. I agreed."

"That's stupid," she says. The words are a bucket of cold water.

"It's not the least bit stupid. You've already left her once."

She swallows and her lip twitches. She squints at the wisteria. When she focuses back on him the skin around her eyes and her forehead is creased. He thinks, this must be the expression she wears when delivering bad news to patients.

"Alex, it was you I left. Not her."

"Same thing."

"No, no." Her foot jiggles frenetically and she presses her palm across her lips as if to stop herself talking. His face stings and there is a plummeting feeling in his stomach. He hears her murmur to herself, "Slow down . . . slow down . . ." and he tells himself the same thing.

"Viorica," he says. "That is all in the past. This is now. Let's talk about now."

Her eyes brighten and she grasps both his hands. "Yes; yes!" she says. She takes a deep breath, releases it, and smiles. He'd forgotten the radiance of her smile. Her body inclines toward his again and she rests a hand on his arm. "I'm almost done with my fellowship, Alex—almost done! I'm an anesthesiologist in all but paperwork now. Can you believe it?"

"Of course I believe it. Of course."

"So my mind is free now, finally—to think, to arrange the—*other* things. To be a full person again, you understand?"

He nods, pulse tripping, skipping beats. "You want more in your life," he says. "Of course."

"Isn't it normal? To want—" she scans the gardens as if looking for words. "To want dinners at home sometimes, and opera maybe, and, and—not being always alone—you understand?"

He nods, wishing his mother were here to hear. *Like a princess you treat her,* his mother said after she moved in. *And in return, she treats you like the frog. You could have had your pick of good women, not a gold-digger scouring the ads in the paper.*

His mother conveniently forgot that it had been her idea to place the ad in the first place. Maybe she'd tired of his complaints during their trans-Atlantic Sunday calls. Once you were in America, people at home seemed to have no tolerance for complaints. "But you can't meet women here like you do in Romania," he'd insist. He'd been in the U.S. eight years at that point, on the upward trajectory he'd mapped for himself. The other engineers were friendly enough at the plant, but invitations for dinner or movies were scarce. He caught himself fantasizing about the packed streetcars in Bucharest, where he'd jostle against some pretty girl and apologize and she'd smile and that would be the start of a conversation. Oh, that press of warm bodies against his own! North Carolina was an empty sea of green: trees everywhere you looked, relenting only for developments, roads, cars. Nothing else. People lived behind the wheel, behind their blinds, behind their desks.

"I am a man without illusions," he'd tell his mother during their Sunday conversations, in the Romanian that slipped over him like a salve. "But still, I have a thing or two to offer a woman." Of course, of course, his mother would agree.

His bank account grew. His waistline grew. He tried bowling with a group from work, but strained his back and had to leave early. His personal ad in the local paper generated a handful of dates, but between his foreign accent and their Southern accents, the encounters spiraled into awkward silence. "They talk and talk and all I hear is mew-mew-mew," he reported to his mother over the phone. Her laughter made him laugh.

"In Romania girls would be tripping over each other to get to meet you," she said. "Maybe American girls are too full of fantasies. Gorged on television. If you looked in Romania you'd find a practical girl without pretensions."

She wasn't wrong. He had more responses in a week to a single ad in the Bucharest paper than to a month's worth of personals in North Carolina. Based on their letters and photographs, he pruned his options down to three: Viorica and the other two.

On their journey out of Bucharest Viorica stuffed her carry-on with pills: for his sugar, for his blood pressure, for his back. A woman without illusions: a practical woman, he told himself. Another woman might have lugged make-up, cheap jewelry, moldy diaries. Not Viorica. "I'll get you healthy; get you exercising," she said as the plane engines gunned. She slid her hand up under his shirt and he squeezed her thigh. She pressed her thumbs into his tight muscles, oblivious to the acne or the hair sprouting between his shoulder blades.

"I understand perfectly," he says to Viorica now. "You're too much alone."

"Yes—yes. I'm a woman, after all. Not just a doctor." She colors.

Alex nods vigorously. They could buy a house together and he could let his mother have the condo. "Not just a woman—you are an *extraordinary* woman," he says, leaning toward her, letting his fingers trace the line of her jaw at last and then drop, lightly brushing her breasts. He feels her nipple harden through the thin cotton of her blouse.

"Let's not exaggerate," she says. "Alex. Listen. There are holes in my life. I miss my Nina. I miss her so it is like a constant pain in my chest. Can you believe I even got myself a cardiogram, but of course it's not my heart—well, not my heart *muscle*. The things they don't teach you in medical school. . . ." Her brief laugh sounds almost like a sneeze.

He's never heard her talk like this before. He doesn't fully buy it, either. If it had been up to her Nina would never have been born. Viorica must be talking about Nina as a veiled way to talk about *them—him* and her.

How lucky he'd been the one home instead of Viorica when the call came about her pregnancy test! When he'd questioned her that night, she'd dissolved into sobs. How could she possibly have a baby as a medical intern? How had this happened? Then the sobs ceased and she lifted her head from the dining table. Black tendrils of hair stuck to her face where the tears had tracked. He'd never seen her more beautiful. "I'll get an abortion," she said.

It felt like a kick to his vocal cords, and he opened and closed his lips like a fish until he could finally draw in enough air to gasp, "No!" and then more loudly, "No, no, I've always wanted a son. A family. Remember my ad? It was in my ad."

"The ad, the damned ad! You want a family *now*? You want me to abandon my training?"

"Let's talk calmly," he'd said, his voice high.

"I can't stop training." The pleading eyes, the flushed cheeks, the tears. She'd pummeled her forehead with her fist.

"Wait. Just—slow down. Let me . . . *think*," he'd cried, and then it came to him. "I could . . . I could ask my mother." And he was able to breathe again as her face cleared, the lines melting into smoothness. "She could get a visa, stay in the extra bedroom for a year or two. Take care of the baby."

"I've really missed my baby," Viorica repeats under the wisteria, looking at him.

"And your baby of course misses *you*, Viorica," he says to her now, leaving it open, ambiguous, just as she has. Her smile is his reward.

"But please call me Vikki," she adds.

"*Vikki?*" His lip curls and her smile freezes. "Vikki?"

She shrugs. "Viorica was too hard for American tongues to pronounce. I changed it. You see, Alex, I *adapt*. I move forward." The implication in her words is a blow to an old bruise, and he grabs her wrist.

"We both adapt," he says. "Who *adapted* to Nina when she

was born, so you didn't fall a day behind in your training?" He's trembling with old anger. As a youth in Bucharest he'd had friends, girlfriends. How has life in North Carolina contracted into two women—his wife, and his mother—two women only? And not even two, if Viorica doesn't mean to come back. His voice drops to a hiss. "Actually, who didn't even *want* Nina in the first place?"

He watches with some satisfaction as her body jerks sideways as if he had physically jabbed her. Her eyes redden. He waits for tears to spill. They don't. In seven years he's seen her cry only that one time.

"We are talking about now, *now,* Alex," she says. She darts up off the bench. "Let's walk." She twists her hand out of his grasp.

She scrambles down the stone steps ahead of him, both hands buried in her pockets. In her black pumps her ankles wobble on the gravel. He's left to trail behind. He begins to see himself as always trailing her. He wonders where this is all headed. He wishes he'd driven his own car to Durham, so he could leave when he wants. His breath is ragged, hot. Sweat beads at his hairline and around his beard. Viorica pauses at the goldfish pond, and he catches up, panting. He wants to talk about the pain in his own chest, the holes in *his* life, his desire, and here they are talking about Nina. His desire has withered anyway, standing beside Viorica looking over the glimmering pond. Nina would love those lily pads, large enough to skip across were she a weightless fairy. Instead, she is chubby like him, with his light wispy hair. Only her gray eyes and dimpled smile favor her mother.

"Are you O.K.?" Viorica says, peering at him. Those eyes through those lashes: a tigress behind the tall grasses of the plains.

"You said let's walk. What if *I* don't want to walk?"

"Fine. Let's sit."

Practical

....

65

"Not there," he says peevishly as she sinks onto a stone bench. "Under—under the magnolia trees."

And again she's ahead of him, gravel crunching under her shoes until they're beneath the spreading arms of the glossy-leafed magnolia.

"In Romania the magnolias were different," he murmurs between panting breaths, and she says, "In Romania everything was different." The sky is mercilessly clear without a hope of shade and he fans himself with his hand. To his surprise she pulls a small foil packet out of her pocket and runs a moist towelette over his brow. His skin tightens as it dries. He nods his gratitude and she says, "I am a neat eater of lobster; I save these from the restaurant." She pats his bulging thigh and says, "So." He waits. She plucks a magnolia leaf from the tree and twirls it in her fingers. "I had three job offers," she begins abruptly, ripping the magnolia leaf into small strips. "I held out for the very best one, and yesterday it came through. High salary, good benefits. But it's in North Dakota, Alex."

He blinks, trying to picture the map of the United States.

"What about North Carolina?"

"No jobs like this one. I'm talking hundreds of thousands of dollars, Alex."

"Is it far?"

"Well. It's a very nice hospital and they need someone fast and the money is very good."

They've been married over seven years. He was thirty-two when he went back to find a wife. She moved into her own place a year ago. It's time for her to come back. Pushing forty, he doesn't have the energy to start at the beginning, yet again.

"You've come to harangue me about a divorce again," he says, hearing his own voice as if squeezed into a vacuum. "I understand now. You're afraid I'll want your money."

She doesn't react.

"That's not the reason I called you," she says.

"Then why?"

"Alex, I want to take Nina with me." Her voice cracks. She sounds tired. The lines around her mouth have deepened and her forehead remains ridged even between frowns.

There's a long, cackling laugh and it takes him a moment to realize it's coming from him. He shakes his head, side to side. How his mother would laugh.

"Nina!" he exclaims, and shakes his head again.

She clutches his arm with both her hands. Her words drop with an unnatural formality, as if they've been rehearsed.

"I will have a house in North Dakota, Alex, with a back yard and swings and she'd have her own room. The schools are good. There's fresh air. This is what a child needs. I have enough to hire a sitter when I have to work outside of school hours, but I've arranged it so at least two days a week I'm done by three. You could visit whenever you wanted and she'd come to you for summers and winter holidays. I'd pay for her travel and for yours."

This isn't in his plan. He will never choose *this*.

"You'll be rich, eh?"

"Be practical, Alex, please." Her fingernails dig into the pale flesh of his underarm and her lips are so close her breath fogs his glasses but he doesn't shift away. "It's time for you to have a life, too. Meet a woman—you need a woman—but how can you with a little girl and an old woman living in your house! It would be good for you to move on. It would be good for Nina, too, to be with her mother."

He can't resist saying, "She could have been with her mother even now."

"I had to work. I had to be practical, get everything lined up just right."

"Everything was lined up just right *before*." He shakes his head. Who told her to keep training training training, to sub-special-ize? Wasn't it enough to be a regular doctor? "You had to be a fancy anesthetist?" he says in English, and hears her mumble, "Anesthesiologist." He shrugs away her hand on his shoulder and stands, walks away. Now she's the one trotting after him. Her voice is high, brittle.

"Alexandru! Please! Wait."

He stops but doesn't turn to her. The truth is, he's a good father but it's been awkward having a little girl and no wife. Sometimes Nina presses herself into his lap, strokes his cheek, wants him to lie down with her so she can fall asleep and he is lost, hot, calls for his mother. Thank God for his mother. Steadfast even with the hateful behavior she's had to weather over the past year. Nina slaps the old woman, kicks her shin. Alex writhes sleepless in his bed some nights, trying to decide how to handle the girl. But what *is* to be done with a child with too much energy? A child who's always scampering ahead, who skips when she should walk, dances when she should skip? His mother blames it on his softness with the girl, on his refusal to spank Nina for misbehavior. But Alex can't bring himself to hit Nina any more than he could ever slap Viorica, even when the most outrageous words flew from her mouth. He's not that kind of man.

"You were a good husband, Alexandru, and the fault was all in me that I couldn't appreciate it," Viorica says. Her words rustle against the vinyl of his jacket. "You have every right to be angry with me. But don't punish Nina. Nina's a little girl who needs her mother. I've worked so hard to make things good for her."

He faces her and says, "You've worked to make things good for you."

She shrugs. Sighs. "Oh Alex," she whispers. "What is so wrong with *that?*"

"How American you've become, *Vikki.*" He watches scarlet spill across her pale cheeks and a bubble of joy rises in his chest. She hangs her head. He reaches out and cups her cheek in his palm, strokes it. He can't help himself and she doesn't pull away. "Was I simply your ticket out?" He's never put into speech the phrase with which his mother hounds him. *You were her ticket out, that's all. Her ticket out.*

When she turns her clear eyes up to him he shivers but there's no way to take back the words. She has never lied—never been anything but brutally direct.

"I answered an ad, Alex," she whispers. "We knew each other a month."

"There was a connection," he insists. She sighs.

"I was first in my class," she murmurs, and he frowns. Her cheek is lifeless against his palm, white again and cold as marble. "In medical school I shared a room with two other students and in winter we slept in shifts because there were two beds and the floor got too drafty. I would have earned two hundred dollars a month in Bucharest." A burr of anger pricks him: she almost seems to have forgotten he is there. He fingers her hair and she closes her eyes for

an instant. He tugs her hair. She doesn't react. A breeze enfolds
them. A small white Scottish terrier bounds around their ankles,
yapping, until an elderly man limps over and snaps a leash to the
dog's collar. Alex shivers at the look in Viorica's eyes when they open
again: the distance across which she seems to not see him at all.

"And yet people back home make a life on two hundred dollars
a month," she continues, as if arguing with herself. "People make
parties, serve drinks, make love. My sister Eva stayed. My mother.
Their letters don't sound unhappy. I send them money, I send them
invitations. Seven years since I saw them. Eva is engaged and in the
photographs she laughs. She's never even met Nina. My mother's
never met her only grandchild."

Viorica blinks hard and seems to come back into herself. She
disentangles his fingers from her hair, and shakes her head. She pats
his arm almost affectionately.

"We gave each other what we needed, didn't we, Alex? For a
time. Please, *please*, let Nina come with me. It would be giving her
what she needs now. It's in your hands. Please." She presses her
palms together as if praying to him.

He hesitates. He tries to imagine the landscape of North Dakota.
If Nina lives with Viorica, he and Viorica will be in constant contact.
There will be telephone conversations, visits. Holidays.

"Please, Alex. It's all up to you. Our lives. Three lives. Please let
her come with me."

Constant contact. Holidays together. There's no need to rush
reconciliation.

"All right," he says slowly. "All right." He's rewarded by an
immediate embrace, her wiry arms warm around his neck, her soft
body pressed briefly against his.

In the car driving to his neighbor's house he begins to feel queasy. He's thinking again of his life as a story: the chapters he'd envisioned, and then the way it's actually been laid down on the page. If he'd married the eighteen-year-old virgin, with her golden hair and her green eyes, she might have cuckolded him by now. On the other hand, that girl had an invalid father, and Alex could have bound her to him by being generous toward her family. She might have settled into having children right away, and not agonized about it, and he might have had a son or two by now. Other men brought over wives who were happy to cook and lie by the pool and spend their husbands' money at the mall.

Viorica hums along with a song on the radio—a song Alex doesn't even recognize. When does she have time to listen to the radio if she works as hard as she says?

They reach the park where the neighbor took Nina and her own five-year-old twins. Viorica sprints from the car before Alex has finished fumbling with the seatbelt. Before he's had time to fully unfold himself from her small Toyota, he hears a high young voice shriek, "Mama!" and sees the blonde blur streak across the sand toward them. He opens his arms but Nina swerves and circles the car and throws herself against Viorica. Viorica stands stiffly, accepting the embrace, her pupils dilated. It needn't have gone like this, Alex tells himself. He's seen Nina sulk and ignore Viorica after a night-duty separation. Nina has been indifferent even to him, when he's returned from a business trip. If she'd been cold toward her mother now, it might have given him grounds to reverse his decision.

The neighbor joins them and Viorica scoops her daughter into her arms. She staggers a little under the girl's weight. Viorica is slim and just over five feet, while Nina, at six, is already four feet tall and weighs sixty pounds. Big-boned, like her grandmother.

"My wife," Alex says to the neighbor, gesturing at Viorica.

"Vikki," Viorica says, letting Nina slide to the ground and extending her hand. The neighbor smiles and looks a little confused.

"I thought you were—away."

"I—have been. I was finishing my training, and now I've—returned. For Nina."

"For me?" and Nina skips around her parents, clapping her hands and yelling, "Hooray—hooray—hooray!"

Alex thanks the neighbor for watching Nina and presses a twenty into her hand, while simultaneously steering Viorica and Nina back toward the car. He's sweating and feels as if a brick has been tied around his neck. Viorica has somehow tricked him, once again. She's engineered everything to happen exactly the way she wants, as it always does. And yet, he can't think of the thing to say to reverse course. The longer he is silent, the harder it becomes. Viorica is describing to Nina the place where they will move, the house she's—already!—made a bid on, the room which she will paint whatever color Nina wants.

"Purple on three sides and pink on one?" Nina asks.

"Yes, all right," Viorica says.

"And purple curtains?"

"O.K. Purple curtains."

"And it'll be you and me?"

"You and me. Yes."

"And daddy will come and visit?"

"O.K. Whenever he wants. Whenever—you want."

"Can he come live there with us?"

Viorica tosses the car keys to Alex and slides into the back seat with Nina. He can't remember the last time she let him drive. She covers Nina's pudgy hand with her own slim fingers. Alex guns the engine.

"No, he can't, sweetheart," Viorica says softly. "Daddy and I don't live together any more."

Alex jerks the car into the flow of traffic on the highway, and Viorcia hisses, "Careful!"

"Who was it who taught you how to drive?" he says.

"Why can't you?" Nina says. "Why can't you live together?"

"Maybe I'd like North Dakota," Alex cuts in from the front seat. He watches Viorica in the rear-view mirror, but she doesn't react. She continues to stroke Nina's hand. "Tell me what your favorite game is now," she says.

"Twister. Do you have a boyfriend?" Nina asks.

"A *what?*" Viorica's head snaps up. She meets Alex's eyes in the rear-view mirror. "How does she know about things like that?" Alex shrugs while Nina says, "I know lots of things. I know what *damned* means and I know where babies come from. Plus my friend Lisa's mommy has a boyfriend. He buys Lisa dolls and she rips the heads off them."

"Tell me, is your teacher very strict at school?"

"Mrs. Kisses?" Nina giggles. "That's what we call her. Mrs. Kissel is her real name. It kind of rhymes. So. *Do* you? Have a boy-friend?"

In the rear-view mirror Alex sees Viorica draw a deep breath. She fumbles with the buttons at her throat. Nina's gray eyes are glued to her mother. Viorica whispers, "I do have a special friend who's a gentleman, Nina."

In the next instant Viorica's head jerks against the front seat as the brakes squeal and Nina is thrown forward against her seatbelt. Horns blare around them and Alex puts up a hand in apology, then slides the car to the break-down lane.

"Are you O.K., baby?" he asks, huffing with the effort of turning in his seat to face Nina. Nina, whimpering now, nods. Viorica rubs her forehead where a walnut-sized lump is rising. "What the hell kind of driving was *that*? Were you watching me or watching the road?" she says in Romanian.

"You didn't say anything about a boyfriend," he says in English. "A *boyfriend*? I thought you—isn't your training everything?"

Viorica's fingertips run over her forehead methodically, examining for a break. In an uncharacteristic rush of words, she cries, "Aren't I entitled to a bit of happiness like everyone else? A scrap of human happiness?" She turns to her daughter, holds her chin between thumb and index finger. "Sweetheart. Sweetheart, don't you want your mother to be happy?"

That's the statement that will most shock Alex's mother much later that evening, once Nina has had her bath and is tucked into her bed and Alex and his mother are savoring shots of vodka after a filling dinner of cabbage stuffed with meat and rice. That a mother can ask such a thing of a six-year-old child! That a mother can so reverse her priorities! His mother will hang on his every word as he describes how calmly he changed his mind, how he saw right then and there that Viorica could never create a suitable home for his daughter, that she would have strange men coming in and out of the picture. He put his foot down and told her what was what. She drove away with her tail between her legs.

His mother will laugh and sip her vodka and nod off in her chair. Alex will stay awake, unable to shake the image of Viorica from his mind. Viorica's fingers entwined around Nina's shoulders so tightly that he had to pry them apart, one by one. Her wild gray eyes, her impotent whisper, "There are lawyers in this country, you know!" He's not afraid of lawyers or their tricks. He'll have only an instant of worry considering Viorica's complete doggedness, her determination in pursuing what she wants. Then he'll pour himself another vodka, adding a splash of orange juice and saying to Viorica's image in his mind, "See, I can be American, too!" And still awake at two in the morning, he'll drape a blanket over his mother. He'll tiptoe into Nina's room to check on her, then head into his own bedroom and lie sideways across his king-size bed, curled in on himself. He'll flip channels on his large-screen, satellite-connected television, searching for the one among the hundreds that will ease him to sleep, then pad out to the kitchen and stand in the glow of the open refrigerator, looking, looking, seeking something to fill the aching hunger in his chest.

Tap Dance

*S*ylvia pulled in a breath and held it to steady her hands, and then firmly pushed the needle again into Mr. Johnson's coffee-colored back at just the spot she had indented seconds earlier with her fingernail. The needle slid in smoothly but she did not feel the familiar "pop."

Mr. Johnson, lying on his side on the bed facing away from her, crooned,

"Oh lawd, lawd, lawd."

"Sorry . . ." Sylvia whispered.

"Are you in?" Ed Vesuvio, the neurology resident, asked. He was watching from the other side of the bed, long arms folded across his chest.

Sylvia sucked in her upper lip, tasting salt. She moved the needle slightly, brows together, squinting at the tube into which the spinal fluid was supposed to flow. The plastic winked emptily at her. Nothing.

"I must be right there," Sylvia said.

"Go a little further."

"Oh, Lawdy!" Mr. Johnson said.

"Now, just a few more seconds, Mr. Johnson," Ed said, raising his voice and speaking slowly, as if addressing a toddler. He bent his 6'2" frame over Mr. Johnson's bed, gripped Mr. Johnson's arms and torso, and gently tucked the old man's head toward his chest, bending the old body further into its fetal position. "You're doing great. Almost done."

Sylvia's cotton shirt had gone cold and damp under her armpits and she suppressed a shudder. She shook a strand of long black hair out of her eyes. She counted vertebrae again, touching each ridge of backbone with her left fingertip while her right hand held the needle in place in Mr. Johnson's back. One, two, three—she was exactly where she was supposed to be, between the second and third lumbars, the portal to the central nervous system. Her needle should have punctured the membranes enclosing the spinal cord, should be draining fluid by now. She inched it forward a millimeter, two.

Nothing.

"You want me to give it a try?" Ed asked from the head of the bed. Sylvia shook her head, avoiding Ed's eye.

"Nah—I haven't missed one of these babies since last year," she said with bravado she wished she felt. In a few months she'd be applying to surgery residency programs, and was counting on a good evaluation from this med school rotation. She continued to maneuver the needle. Long behind her were the days when her skin went cold and clammy as she drew blood from a patient, or her head spun and black flecks obscured her vision. How humiliating it had been to sink to the floor to avoid passing out. "Taps are my specialty. I'll get it," she said to Ed.

"Thatta girl. Not a quitter—I like that," Ed said, and Sylvia felt a
rush of adrenaline. She stole a glance at him, and he winked at her.
Flushing, she squinted back at the needle, at Mr. Johnson's back.

"So, were you a natural at procedures when you were a student?"
she asked Ed as she inched the needle forward, lifting her voice
above Mr. Johnson's soft moans. "Were you one of those star students
who knew how to kid around even their first time in the O.R.?"

"I've always liked procedures," he said. "Good with my hands.
It's a guy thing. Plus, I'd been around stuff before, y'know, helping
my dad do sutures when I was in high school, stuff like that. Hung
around his orthopedics office."

"A guy thing indeed," Sylvia said, lifting her eyes momentarily
from the needle to make a face at him. He smiled. Her fingers
trembled as she wiggled the spinal tap needle. She hated that her
fingers trembled. She hated that she'd had to learn to steel herself,
to control her breathing and flush all thoughts from her mind.
Sometimes she even mouthed a silent prayer, *please God, please God
let me get through this.* Not that she was a religious person, but it
seemed to help, for now she had a reputation as the student who did
not let people down. She would get the fluid, make the incision—do
whatever was needed. She could do it every time but the first.

With a sharp bump and a scraping sound Sylvia's needle stopped.
"Damn," she breathed. "I think I hit bone."

"Uumnph," sighed Mr. Johnson.

"O.K., pull out. Pull out. We'll start over."

Her heart shivered in her chest and sent her pulse thudding into
her temples. She'd screwed up. Into her mind popped the saying
she'd heard from surgery residents: *When you're swimming with
sharks, don't bleed.* Ed would never say such a thing. She slid the

needle out of Mr. Johnson's back and in the same fluid motion wedged a cotton ball directly over the spot where the needle had been.

"Almost done now, Mr. Johnson!" she called out, trying to match the cheerful lilts the resident doctors used. Mr. Johnson moaned.

"You take a rest now, sir, before we give it another go," Ed said, patting the old man on the shoulder. He came around to Sylvia's side of the bed. He laid both hands against Mr. Johnson's back and sought out the same landmarks Sylvia had used: the hills and valleys of the spinal column. Mr. Johnson's wrinkled skin was slack and dry, sprouting curly white hairs unevenly along his back.

"Do you think you might have gone in a little slanted?" Ed asked Sylvia. His brown eyes searched her face. The musky scent of his after-shave stirred a memory of her first college boyfriend. Was it Old Copenhagen? Grey Flannel? Most residents didn't wear after-shave, as far as she could tell. But then, neither did most residents wear Ed's funky ties with bright geometric patterns, crisply pressed Perry Ellis pants or the sharp white designer shirts—clothes that would have camouflaged him in a glossy fashion magazine. In the V.A. hospital in Durham, North Carolina, they made him stand out. You didn't see *him* in button-down Oxford shirts and wrinkled khakis, like the other residents. The medical students called him "Dapper Dan" behind his back. But he was also known for always coming prepared to journal club, for his technical skills, and for being the chairman's favored choice for chief resident next year.

She'd been minutes away from hearing about where he'd grown up when the call came about Mr. Johnson. They'd been headed to dinner in the hospital cafeteria. It was their first night on call

together and only the third day of the rotation. They leaned shoulder
to shoulder against the tile wall in the corridor outside the ER while
Ed answered the page, rolling his eyes as he listened. He turned to
Sylvia and gave her a monotone summary: Elderly black man. Sixty-
seven, history of stroke, found wandering about in a confused state
at his nursing home. Dumped off by private ambulance; no medical
records with him. Disoriented. No fever, but altered mental status all
the same. Family not available.

Her mind raced to keep up with the casual dropping of facts.
It reminded her of the way the children of the wealthy at her high
school would drop names, and she'd have to prepare in advance to
keep up.

Altered mental status, Ed had repeated, pausing and looking
expectantly at her.

Rule out meningitis, she'd said, right on cue. Rule out meningitis,
of course. A whole big work-up. Which meant starting with a lumbar puncture, or spinal tap.

Before dinner. Before Sylvia got to discover anything about Ed
that she didn't already know from hospital gossip.

In the elevator Ed asked her, "You wanna do the tap?" and something in his tone made her spirits rise. "You want it, it's yours." It had
felt like a gift.

His voice now was even and flat as he asked, had she gone in
slanted.

"I thought I was in perfectly straight," she finally said. "It's
him—he's not right. His back's all—weird." To her great mortifica-
tion she felt her face burn. But Ed's direct gaze had already flitted
to Mr. Johnson's exposed back. How Mr. Johnson had giggled and

squirmed when she pulled up his light blue pajama top and pulled down the elastic waist of his pajama bottom. He'd laughed and wiggled while she prepped a large rectangle of his skin with Betadine. One, two, three neat swoops with a cold wet sponge, to thoroughly disinfect before introducing the needle: she could do it in her sleep. Ed's eyes coursed over Mr. Johnson's back, then skimmed the chucks placed neatly underneath him to protect the bed linens. He inspected the needle and tubing, nodding now and then.

"I hear you wanna go into surgery, maybe neuro," he said.

"How'd you hear that?"

"Oh, y'know, people talk, word gets around." He winked at her. "You've got quite the reputation as star student, y'know."

Heat shot through her chest and up into her neck. "Well, I work really hard."

"Same thing." They smiled together.

"Y'know, sometimes patients just don't cooperate," he added. She blinked, having forgotten for a moment that anyone else was in the room. "You ready for another try? Let's go." Ed rubbed his hands together, and laid a hand on Mr. Johnson's shoulder. Sylvia swallowed. He nodded toward the lumbar puncture tray. She couldn't believe it—he was giving her another chance! Her muscles went weak with relief.

"Mr. Johnson?" Ed's voice rose. "We need to give that spinal tap one more go. O.K., sir?"

There was no answer. Ed cocked his head and repeated his question, louder. Silence. He frowned at Sylvia. Sylvia shrugged. Ed leaned over the bed, peering into Mr. Johnson's face, and then squatted back down on his haunches beside Sylvia, grinning.

"He's asleep," he whispered. He chuckled. "That's our cue to go!"

Sylvia hesitated, thinking for a moment about a small group discussion she'd participated in just last week about informed consent.
Ed nodded, drumming his fingers on the side of the bed. She pulled
on fresh sterile gloves, felt a tremor pass through her hands, shook
them. Then she carefully walked her fingers down Mr. Johnson's
backbone, counting as she went.

"L-1, L-2, L-3—right there," she said, naming each vertebra. Ed's
fingers traced her path.

"Right," he said, his hand cupping hers for an instant before it
moved away. The small tiled room pressed in on her.

Her thumbnail left a new crescent-moon imprint in Mr. Johnson's
skin. She put a fresh needle on her set-up. She was sweating but
it was too late to remove her white coat. Her heart hammered in
her chest. She wanted to check the expression on Ed's face, to see
whether he looked worried about her approach or unconcerned, but
he was out of sight, just behind her. She mouthed *Thank you God*
when she saw how completely steady her hands were, how stable
they remained as she pushed the needle into the brown back before
her. The next moment there was a loud yelp and Ed sprang to his
feet, his knee knocking into her back as he scrambled to steady Mr.
Johnson.

"Whoa there, sir! Now let's stay on our side. We don't want to
roll backward onto that needle, do we?"

"Oh, lawdy, lawd lawd!" The voice was high-pitched and full of air.

"I know, I know," Ed said soothingly, but Sylvia caught him rolling his eyes as he said it. Her face burned again as she smiled at him.
It was the two of them now, the two of them against that damned

spinal fluid that was trying to ruin their night. She swallowed. Then she focused her entire attention on the needle she held. Mr. Johnson flashed before her and disappeared. Only she, the needle, and Ed's eyes existed. And some skin: some brown, slightly damp, sagging skin. Millimeter by millimeter the needle slid in. She held her breath, waiting for the curl of fluid, watching, praying, and—

"Nothing," she sighed after a few moments. "Nothing. I just don't get it." Her voice cracked.

"Try a little to the left, or the right."

"I did. I've been moving it all *over* the place in here—"

"Yow!"

"Damn. He made me pop out."

"Sir, you gotta help us out here. If you're not real still, it makes it all take longer, makes us have to do extra tries, and you don't want that, do you?" Ed shook Mr. Johnson's shoulder. "It's probably the anatomy," he murmured to Sylvia, squatting again beside her to help clean up the tray. "These old guys, sometimes their backs are all messed up from old injuries and it's real hard to get in there. Your technique was perfect. All right, let's get this thing done and get to dinner before they run out of chocolate chip cookies."

She nodded. The electrical excitement had drained from her body. Star student indeed. Her neck was damp with sweat. As she switched places with Ed, she caught a glimpse of herself in the mirror over the sink. Her shoulders stooped forward. The pockets of her white jacket bulged with reference handbooks and reflex hammers and extra syringes. Flyaway strands of the bangs she was trying to grow out hung in front of her eyes. She pulled back her elbow-length hair and twisted it into a knot, then groped in her pocket for a rubber band.

"Are you ready?" Ed said. She spun around, coloring, nodding. She should have just put her hair up in the morning, instead of having to mess with it, giving Ed the unnecessary reminder that she was female. Ed cleared his throat. "O.K. then, here goes."

Her stomach lurched, and then made a loud gurgling noise. To her horror, Ed said, "Hungry?"

"You heard that?"

"Well, give me ten minutes, twenty tops, and I'll have us on our way to dinner."

She nodded again. Her muscles quivered. She glanced at her watch: 9:00. She had skipped lunch to finish chart notes on all her patients, which were always at least a page each. After fourteen hours of fasting, what was another twenty minutes?

"O.K.—I'm ready to see the master at work," she said. But he motioned toward the other side of the bed.

"I need you to position him," he said. Usually they only had to hold children and infants. She gritted her teeth. This old man—this old lump of flesh, barely conscious of his life—could this be called living? Probably nothing more they could do for him anyway—and here they were spending the better part of an evening on him. Instead of sitting side by side at dinner, their heads bent over the neuro atlas, Ed's hands tracing the cranial nerves for her.

She shrugged off her heavy white jacket and draped it over the chair next to Mr. Johnson's bed. As the air conditioning cooled the sweat on her arms, she shivered, and then the goose bumps on Mr. Johnson's arms caught her eye. She bit her lip and pulled the blanket over his legs. She rolled Mr. Johnson onto his side, pulling against him to hold him in place, patting his shoulder. She looked into his face for the first time. His eyes were shut. His cheeks were peppered with white razor stubble just like her grandfather's had been. She'd refused to kiss her grandfather when she was little because his face scratched hers.

She suppressed an unexpected urge to touch Mr. Johnson's face. She cleared her throat. "Mr. Johnson? Dr. Vesuvio is going to do that spinal tap now."

Mr. Johnson abruptly sat up, scattering equipment that Ed had rested on his prone body. His arm swung out and toppled the water pitcher on his bedside table. Sylvia sprang out of the way as water slapped the floor. Her nostrils flared.

"Whoa—where are you going? Please keep still. We have to—"

"Huh? The devil . . . I thought you gone and done it awready!"

Ed's eyebrows slid up and he straightened, exchanging glances with Sylvia.

"That was the first clear thing he's said all evening," Ed said. Sylvia caught Mr. Johnson by both wrists and tried to flatten him back onto his bed, but he resisted.

"He's stronger than he looks," she said.

"Mr. Johnson? Can you tell me what year it is, sir?" Ed said. The man stopped struggling against Sylvia and his eyes widened.

"The *year*?" He made it a two-syllable word. "You don't know the damn year?"

He's clearing, Sylvia thought. He doesn't need the tap.

"Can you just say it, please?"

Silence. Sylvia held her breath.

"Mr. Johnson. The year?"

"Two thousand?"

"Yes, that's right. And where are we?"

A chuckle from Mr. Johnson.

"Where we at?"

"Yes. Where are we at?"

"Any fool could see that!"

Sylvia suppressed a smile. Hope bubbled in her chest. Maybe they'd get to dinner soon. She'd have other chances to confirm Ed's impression of her star student status.

Ed rolled his eyes but his voice remained even.

"Yes, all right, Mr. Johnson. I know any fool can see it, but can *you* tell *me*? Sir? *Where are we at?*" The firm, commanding tone. *Answer.* "Mr. Johnson? Where are we, sir? I need an answer, *now*!"

Pause.

"Lawdy, lawd lawd lawd!" he stammered, sinking back onto the bed.

Sylvia and Ed sighed together.

"All right. He's just bought himself a tap." Ed squared his jaw and his eyes looked flinty. He knelt on the floor beside the bed and uncapped his syringe. Sylvia repositioned Mr. Johnson, holding his thin, sinewy arms. His skin was so loose it seemed like a duvet cover, tethered to nothing beneath. He didn't resist her grasp. His toothless mouth was puckered, but a small smile flickered on his lips. His eyes were open but the milky irises focused beyond her. Sometimes the vets flirted with her, but he seemed engrossed in the paint peeling underneath the windowsill. His face was an abandoned window. If he'd had passions, a family, ambitions, none of those existed in this room at this moment. He was a vacant body on a foam mattress on a metal bed.

The white stubble on his head matched that on his cheeks. He

looked older than sixty-seven. Much older than her sixty-year-old
father, but then, her father spent every fourth Sunday night sitting
on the closed toilet lid in their one bathroom, reading a Hungarian
newspaper and waiting for the jet-black dye on his hair and eyebrows to set. "If you have a foreign accent *and* white hair, they'll fire
you for sure!" he'd sometimes tell Sylvia. Her father had earned a
Ph.D. in biology in Hungary. In Boston he'd worked his way up
from glassware washer to technician to assistant in the lab.

"Of course, if you are a doctor, no one cares if your hair is white
or where you were born. They need you," her father would continue.
"A medical degree is your international passport. Look at Adam
Tamas—who you know as Adam Thomas, of course. Finished
third-to-last in his medical school class in Budapest but now delivering babies at the Brigham and living in a semi-attached house in
Brookline."

"Who needs a house in Brookline?" Sylvia would retort. But
if her mother heard that, she'd chime in, her voice soft, beseech-
ing. "Ah, but think of the people you could help. The people you'd
save. What could be more satisfying than that? *Saving lives, Sylvia.*
You'll get over the queasiness about blood. Everyone does. Master
your feelings. Put them away. Once you learn to get used to blood,
cut incisions, use the instruments, nothing's hard. Then you can be
somebody."

Sylvia watched Ed prep Mr. Johnson. Those smooth square
hands had neatly trimmed oval fingernails. Unlined, elegant hands.
They moved swiftly, with assurance. They were a pianist's hands
caressing the keys of a collapsing body. A painter's hands flying
over a canvas. He hummed a melody she didn't recognize, as if he

were merely whitewashing a wall. A fringe of dark hair fell toward his eyes. Her hands itched to brush it out of his way, but they were occupied with Mr. Johnson. Ed tossed his head and his hair fell into place. Sylvia shook her own head. What had she been thinking? How weird it would have seemed if she'd actually touched Ed's forehead. But she'd experienced this before: the erotic charge among the workers at the end of a code, the longing for the surgeon at the head of the heart patient's operating table. There was something about gathering with young, healthy people beside a dying, older person. It made you yearn for those still standing: made you want them, love them, when you hardly knew them.

"Here we go!" sang Ed as his needle entered Mr. Johnson's back.

"Ow! Mary mother of God!" Mr. Johnson yelled. Sylvia's heart flipped in her chest, and she leaned over Mr. Johnson, toward Ed. Surely, surely, they had spinal fluid this time? Surely they were almost done? She asked the question with her eyes. Ed caught her expression and said, "You like basketball, Sylvia?"

"Basketball?" She frowned, feeling unsteady.

"Yeah."

"Basketball. I—um—I've become a big Duke fan since I've been here," she stammered.

"Lawd lawd lawd!" said Mr. Johnson.

"I've got tickets to the first three games," Ed said, looking not at her but at the procedure he was performing. She imagined he was measuring the height of the column of spinal fluid, to determine if it was under normal pressure. She marveled at his ability to do that while discussing sports.

"Henderson gave them to me—he has a season pass," Ed continued.

"Must be nice to be buddies with the department chair," she said, struggling to match his light, bantering tone. Another skill she needed to master if she were to succeed in the operating room.

"Nah—he's just an old med school buddy of my dad's," he said.

That must be nice too, she thought, but she said nothing. He continued, "Maybe we could—"

"Lawd, man!" Mr. Johnson yelled.

She saw Ed's eyebrows crimp together. Beads of sweat dotted his upper lip.

"Hmmm—"

"In?" she asked.

"Strange—I *should* be in—"

"Stop!" Mr. Johnson whimpered. "You there! You! Stop! For gawd's sake, please. Stop!"

Sylvia held the old man's arms.

"Are you in?" she repeated, her voice wobbling. Ed didn't look at her.

"It must be the anatomy," he said, sighing and getting to his feet. "I haven't missed one in years!" His jaw worked as he paced the cubicle of a room. The fluorescent light above the bed buzzed. Sylvia looked longingly at the oak door leading out. Perhaps if they could just let in some air . . .

"He doesn't have a fever," Sylvia murmured. "Couldn't we just . . . umm . . ."

Ed frowned. "The elderly don't always get fevers, even with meningitis."

Sylvia wanted to say, *Why don't we get some dinner and try again later.* Or, *Maybe we should get some X-rays, see why we're having so much trouble.* But Ed must have considered that, rejected it. She wanted to ask, *Do we really need to get this lumbar puncture at all tonight? If we think it might be meningitis, can't we just treat him with antibiotics as if it is?* But that was probably a dumb question. Her stomach was so tight with hunger that she couldn't think straight. How was she going to be a surgeon if her thoughts drifted toward dinner instead of focusing on Mr. Johnson and the differential diagnosis of altered mental status?

She said, "Anything I can do to help?"

Ed took off his white coat. Unlike hers, it was calf-length and had his name embroidered on the right breast pocket. A straight iron crease ran down each arm. He unbuttoned his cuffs and rolled his shirt sleeves up to his elbows. His biceps and deltoids were beautifully defined; maybe he'd played varsity basketball himself? He was tall enough. Was he dating anyone? Sylvia colored. She bent her thoughts back toward altered mental status.

"I need you to curl him more," Ed said, looking directly into her eyes. His pupils were constricted, his voice urgent, his forehead creased. Something in the room changed. Her mouth went dry.

Her pulse picked up as all at once she understood. They were a team now. Unstoppable. They were up against obstacles, crisis perhaps, but they'd keep trying, pushing, working that needle, no matter how late it got or how tired or hungry they might become. They would get this damned spinal fluid and accept nothing less, even if it took all night.

American Dreaming

....

90

"Curl him as much as you can. Let's open up those damned spaces between the vertebrae."

She looked at Mr. Johnson. He had completely straightened his spine and was sprawled across the bed, muttering to himself.

"Sir, I need you to get on your side again," she said in a loud, firm voice.

"Oh no no no no no!" he wailed.

"Yes—c'mon—yes—we're—almost—done—come *on*—" and she fought against his body on the bed, surprised at the leaden weight of each limb.

"Need help?" Ed asked, tearing the wrap from a fresh lumbar puncture tray.

"No, I'm fine," she said. "Oh Mr. Johnson—PLEASE!" for he had slumped onto his back again. A pulse of anger stabbed Sylvia's ribcage. Her stomach growled. She filled with savage strength. "This is for your own good!" She shoved her shoulder into his back one more time, rolling him onto his side, then scurried to the other side of the bed and hooked one arm under his knees. With her free hand she grabbed both his wrists. She pulled him together as if shutting an accordion. He moaned, burped, then giggled.

"This is not funny!" She wanted to slap him.

"That's great!" Ed called. "Hold him just like that!"

Ed disappeared. Her field of vision narrowed to Mr. Johnson's pale pajamas. With all her strength, she held him curled in his fetal pose. His breath washed over her, damp and slightly sweet-smelling. There was another smell too, faint, of urine. She closed her eyes. The darkness behind her eyelids brought back sitting in art history, learning how master painters studied anatomy. The cool dark lecture hall, the slides dancing across the screen. The laser pointer tracing brush strokes. The professor invited her to take his senior seminar on Renaissance Masters, but it conflicted with a pre-med requirement. Where would she be now, this very instant, if she'd taken that senior seminar? She squeezed her eyes open. What would she ever have done with an art history degree?

Her back and both arms ached.

"I'm in—any second now—" Ed called from the other side of the bed. His voice had a tight brassy quality to it. "Awww—Mother fucker!"

"Lawdy lawd lawd!"

"Ed?"

"Nothing. Got some blood. Don't know where the hell I am now."

Maybe we should stop for the night, Sylvia said silently. *Maybe we should get a CT scan before trying again. Maybe we should just start antibiotics.* But if these ideas came to *her,* surely Ed had considered and rejected them? A senior resident, considered among the best. The resident chosen to receive the chairman's basketball tickets. She felt an uncomfortable burning in her chest, and her breath came fast. Surely Ed would stop if that was the right thing to do?

Her life had telescoped into one small green-tiled room and two men: one prone, disintegrating before her eyes, and the other tall and vibrant, full of energy and knowledge. Who could blame her for siding with one against the other?

"Keep holding him like that."

"O.K."

"Ow!—"

American Dreaming

....

92

"I can get it." His voice cracked and a warm tenderness bulleted from her middle into her chest. He sounded younger, uncertain. He needed her.

"I know you can get it," she heard herself say.

"Any minute. We'll get it any minute now."

"Yes. Yes. I know we will."

They went on until almost midnight. Ed had to separate the lumbar trays into two piles because they couldn't stuff them all into one biohazard container.

After, they sat side by side in the physicians' on call lounge, next to the vending machines, eating Cheetos and Milky Way bars. The cafeteria had closed at 11:30. Sylvia's stomach churned. A burning rose in her throat after each swallow. In Ed's tousled hair, in the stony, silent way he stared at the floor, Sylvia thought she read his regret. But she couldn't get out of her mind the image of two pale tracks snaking their way down Mr. Johnson's face when they'd finally left him: the salty residue of his tears.

"You can go home. It's quiet now," Ed said softly at last, nudging Sylvia's shoulder with his. She shivered. "You don't need to spend the night."

She pictured the twenty-minute drive down deserted moonless roads to her empty apartment: miles where her high beams picked out nothing but spindly pines and the occasional glow of a deer's eyes. Her college boyfriend hadn't been able to suppress a guffaw when she asked if he'd consider moving to North Carolina with her. He broke up with her two months before graduation, because what was the point of continuing?

"It's all right. By the time I get home, it'll be time to turn back and come in to round anyway," Sylvia said to Ed.

"Thanks for your help. Damn hard LP. Must've been the anatomy."

She swallowed. "No problem," she said.

"Sylvia." Ed grabbed her sleeve as she rose for the on-call room. He squinted. "I—I, ah, wouldn't mention in the morning how many attempts we made. Probably we should've stopped after I gave it a good try." Her stomach tightened. A good try? How many was a good try? Two? Four? The fine hairs on the back of her neck bristled.

"You mean," she began.

"No—it's cool. Everything's fine. But—let's keep it between just you and me, eh?" It didn't sound like a question. He squinted more.

She nodded. She couldn't say anything. It was hard to look at him.

In the morning X-rays confirmed that Mr. Johnson had had several back surgeries, fusing his spinal column in ways that didn't readily allow needles inside. Spinal fluid was removed under X-ray guidance. There was no meningitis.

"Aha! The anatomy, just as we suspected!" Ed said triumphantly. He gave Sylvia a wide smile.

She focused on his hands. How beautiful she had thought them the night before. They were freshly scrubbed, nails neatly trimmed. Delicate hands, but strong. A quarterback's hands. A frat boy's hands. Not gnarled and veined and calloused like Mr. Johnson's hands. The hands of a rich man, a man who's arrived. A man who lives in a detached house in Brookline.

A butcher's hands.

"Wanna grab some breakfast after rounds?" he asked her brightly.

"I—I'm just gonna get a cup of coffee and catch up on some reading," she mumbled. He studied her for a moment, then shrugged. He spun on his heel and clapped Thomas, their pharmacy student, on the back.

"You a basketball fan, Tommy, m'man?" she heard him ask.

She looked down at her own hands, which were trembling. They looked small, dimpled at the knuckles. Nails bitten to the quick. Where would these hands take her? She heard the elevator bing, and veered toward it. A noisy cluster of people exited: a heavy-set middle-aged black woman, dressed in a flowery print dress and a broad-rimmed straw hat, and three children of varying ages.

" . . . if he doesn't recognize you, don't you worry none," the woman was saying. "Grandpa Johnson had a rough night, a rough night, but thank the Lord they got him here so they can make him all better, so he can play with y'all again."

Sylvia froze at the elevator, hand against the rubber of the doors to keep them from closing. She listened to the children's voices as they receded down the hallway.

"Will he make us them biscuits shaped like dogs again?" the littlest boy asked.

"I don't know about that, sugar, but I know he'd love to if he could. He didn't miss a single Sunday making 'em for me when I was a little girl."

People filed into the elevator around Sylvia and still she stood there, straining to hear.

"I gotta show him how good I whistle now," another child was saying. "Will he . . ."

And they disappeared around a corner, a flurry of arms and legs and high-pitched questions, and Sylvia leaned into the elevator and pressed her back against the metal rear wall, letting other people hit the buttons. She'd ride up, down, wherever. She bit her lips, dug her fingernails into her arms—anything she could do to keep the tears from coming. She had to jab at her eyes once during her walk in the underground tunnel to her car, but as she sank into the seat and turned the key in the ignition, a wave of fatigue swept over her and doused her urge to cry. By the time she hit the highway, she was fiddling with the radio controls in search of news, squinting against the wind sweeping through the wide open windows, and fighting hard just to stay awake.

Waiting for Power

*A*nd anyway, which is worse? Alice thinks, and her jaw clenches because it is a thought she has not had in nearly two years, a thought she believed she'd never have again. She certainly had not thought it when she issued the invitation, standing with Ian on her back porch in the litter from the storm. Tree limbs as thick as her waist had iced over and snapped as if they were asparagus shoots. The crashes had shattered her sleep three nights before, but the roof she installed last summer withstood the blows.

She does not think, *which is worse,* until she is across from Ian at the kitchen table: alone with Ian because the Romanians have disappeared. Outside, the mercury still hovers at thirty, unseasonably cold for this far south.

Just ten minutes earlier she was savoring her second cup of coffee, absorbing its lovely heat into her cupped hands. This first full day of restored power was unfurling at holiday pace. Alice slouched in her chair, bringing herself eye-level with the Trandafir kids like she does with the third-graders she teaches, so her height wouldn't intimidate them. The boys had started to answer her questions, too, until Rex began his frantic barking, lunging from one window to the next. In his brief pauses Alice heard the hum of the Vespa, then watched Ian's hulking frame, ridiculously large on the small red bike, bounce over the ice on her driveway. Sighing, she rose to get the door. The Trandafirs sprang up too, the boys still holding half-eaten toast spread with jam. The father, Simon, stammered, "Ah—we interfere with your day—we go back upstairs . . ."

"Nonsense! It's just my ex—please eat!" Seeing the blank expressions on their faces, she added, "my former husband," speaking more slowly so they'd understand.

She pulled on her son's old parka while Rex flew down the porch stairs, tail wagging, no longer barking. He jumped up in greeting as Ian slid off his helmet and shook out his chin-length chestnut hair. Alice suppressed an impulse to brush the graying wisps out of his eyes, like she used to do.

"I called but couldn't get through, so I thought to stop by and make sure you were all right."

"I'm fine. No phone yet but my power's back."

"I wanted to check on you. Make sure."

Alice combed her long fingers through her own unbrushed hair and looked down at her slippers. Pale pink terrycloth, oversized, they looked like a child's. The icy air fingered her bare ankles and she stamped her feet.

"Yeah—thanks," she murmured.

"It's good you're safe and warm. I'm still in the cold." He looked past her into the kitchen. "You have guests?"

"I took in the Trandafirs. You know—the tenants in that basement apartment of Letty's across the street. She's away in Cancun, lucky devil, but that side of the street is still without power. I put them in the kids' old rooms."

"Ever the do-gooder," he said.

She shrugged. "Last night was kind of nice, actually—having a full house again. We lit candles. We cooked a big pot of spaghetti. I had nothing else in the house."

Ian examined the ruined trees. Loblolly pine trunks stood like schoolchildren's pencils, capped by sharpened yellow tips instead of leafy tops. Ian rubbed ice crystals from his mustache and Alice noticed the redness in his cheeks. Maybe it was simply from the cold.

His gaze arched from the treetops down to the dogwoods he'd planted fifteen years ago, just behind the house. They now bent like weeping willows toward the ground. Alice felt a stab of sorrow as she recalled a tanned, broad-shouldered Ian, muscles barely plumping with the effort of excavating pits for those dogwood root bundles while their two young sons and Chip (a former Rex, long since deceased) hopped with anticipation around his feet. Her eyes refocused and fifty-five-year-old Ian reappeared, ski jacket ballooning around his thin frame, the skin on his face thickened, cross-hatched with lines. His hands trembled slightly—or was his whole body shivering? It *was* freezing, after all. Ian caught her eye and held it.

"If you need a place to stay you can camp out on the couch," she mumbled, shuffling back into the house. He followed without pause.

Alice's head went light for a nauseating instant when they stepped into the empty kitchen, cleared of all breakfast dishes except hers. Ian hung his jacket on the hook that had been his, beside the door, stepped out of his boots at exactly his old spot on the doormat, and straightened the framed photo of their sons that always tilted to the right. As if he'd never left. Alice braced herself against the kitchen counter and tried to clear her throat. A sudden tinkling crash, like broken crystal, drew Rex, barking, toward the windows. The foot-long icicles under the eaves were starting to detach and shatter. It was warming. The spinning in her head stopped and she dropped into a chair cattycorner to Ian at the kitchen table. His power would return. He'd go.

And if he doesn't? She watches him pour coffee, top off hers. He's started in on a story Alice can't follow, about his secretary and departmental politics.

If he doesn't go?

Thirteen months ago she'd held her ground against his pleading, feeling frozen, biting the inside of her cheek until it bled. But now, Alice harbors slivers of the desolation that invaded her the first stormy night. Her hands are chapped and her back aches from the wood she hauled to keep a fire going her own forty-eight hours without power. How bleak those nights were, when darkness fell at five o'clock! How utterly alone she felt as she pressed close to the fireplace, squinting to read, checking her watch every twenty minutes to see if it was late enough yet to crawl into bed. If he'd been with her. . . . Which is worse?

She shakes her head, and when Ian asks "What?" she realizes her lips have been moving.

"Nothing." She stands, dumps the rest of her coffee down the disposal. "I—have to get dressed."

"So tell me about the Romanians." Ian lifts his bushy eyebrows and turns the velvet brown intensity of his eyes on her.

"I didn't get much—they barely speak English." She shrugs.
"Or perhaps it's your shyness," he says, a sparkle in his eye, smiling.
She brushes crumbs off the table. "It could be me, I guess."

It turns out, of course, that Simon's English is better than Alice
realized, and in the evening on her sofa in front of the fire he and
Ian carry on a lively discussion of Eastern Orthodox religions. In
the large, airy kitchen, Alice and Simon's wife Aurica clear dishes
from the Indian curry dinner Ian whipped up. When they were
married her friends envied her Ian's flair in the kitchen. These days,
Alice often opens a can of soup in the evening and pops bread in
the toaster. The soft, cellophane-bagged American loaf keeps longer
than the fancier baguettes Ian favored.

Simon, a nearly bald, spectacled man with a twitch in the corner
of his mouth, has shed his self-consciousness of the night before.
Ian has that effect on people, and tonight he is in top form: funny,
charming, the perfect raconteur.

"Back when I was chair of religious studies at the Div school," he
is saying, and Alice sees Simon's forehead wrinkle. He shushes his
sons, who are laughing as they play tag with the dog, spilling around
the sofa in a way that makes Alice's heart swell.

"Chair? Please—you say, ah, *chair*—" Simon's expression untan-
gles into comprehension, then admiration. "Ah—chair*man*? You are
chairman!"

"Was. Stepped down a year ago—had done it long enough," and
Ian brushes the air dismissively while Alice thinks, yeah, *that's* why
you stepped down.

"But back when I was chair, one summer I took the family to
tour the Eastern European countries. Remember, Ally? The wall

had come down, dictatorships were crumbling. I wanted you all to get to see. Czechoslovakia, Poland, Hungary—I never did get us to Romania, though. Very interesting places, those. Fascinating religious similarities and divergences."

"Well, being scientist, I am atheist, of course," Simon says.

"What do you mean, being a scientist?"

"How men of science can believe, when we know laws of nature?"

"Ah—I would argue the two are not incompatible world views," Ian says, waggling his bottle of alcohol-free beer to emphasize his point. "In fact, I can give you an article I wrote about God and science, published in the *Atlantic,* reprinted in a divinity textbook last fall. I gave Alice a copy."

Alice ignores the hint that she produce the book. Aurica slides beside her husband on the sofa, and both Trandafirs lean toward Ian like flowers. Alice stifles a yawn and turns to the boys, who've resumed their game of tag but silently this time, circling the kitchen table on tiptoe, cheeks puffed in demonic suppressed smiles.

"How about some ice cream or brownies or something? I stocked up today. I'm prepared."

Alice speaks softly but Aurica hears and trips over Simon's long legs in her rush to return to the kitchen.

"No—please—I help, I help—thank you very much—you, please, *you* must sit on couch, please—" Her translucent skin is stippled pink.

"Oh, for heaven's sake! I don't need to hear Ian's tales—let me feed your two lovely boys. They remind me of mine. Except—mine are already in college."

Aurica falters, lips parted.

"Boys, yes, they're . . ." she says with a small laugh, but her green eyes slide as if involuntarily toward Ian, and Alice feels a surprising jolt of the old jealousy. Its slow burn rises from her middle into her cheeks, and she works to neutralize the expression on her face, then catches herself and mutters, "as if anyone's looking at *me* these days!"

"Please?" Aurica says, twisting her hands.

"Oh—a liability of living alone—talking to yourself!" Alice says lightly, then reads confusion on Aurica's face. "Go on, I've got this under control. Go . . . *enjoy.* Ian tells a great story."

Aurica reddens to her scalp, making Alice wonder why she used that tone of voice. She digs the ice cream scoop into the hardened chocolate brownie with renewed force, thinking, *This is not who I am. The woman Ian makes me is not the woman I am.* Aurica hovers over her children, handing out napkins and spoons when the table is already set with these, talking in hushed Slavic-sounding syllables. Above the waistband of her too-tight jeans a roll of flesh bulges each time she reaches over the table, and she self-consciously tugs down her sweater. Alice thinks, *She's like a plump peach, and I'm like an autumn leaf, drying into brittleness.* She smirks at the thought. Aurica is out of things to distribute, and awkwardly folds her arms across her chest.

"He is very smart man, your husband," Aurica says. "Has traveled much, written much, and thinks about each thing, how you say, *deeply* . . ."

"He is not my husband anymore. And there are other qualities that make a good husband, as I'm sure you know."

Aurica gives an uncertain half-nod, then turns to the sink and starts to towel dry the pots that are draining upside down in the drying rack.

"But—yes—he's a very smart, very charming, man," Alice echoes uncertainly, and neither speaks again as Ian's voice fills the room.

There was an awkward moment around ten o'clock when the Trandafirs realized Ian would be staying on the couch. Alice tried to herd them up to their rooms, but Ian stubbornly immobilized them with his stories. When Alice's yawns became authentic, she gathered an armload of blankets and a pillow from the hall closet and dumped them unceremoniously on the living room sofa. At once, Simon shot to his feet and volunteered himself and Aurica for the living room—the floor was fine for them, Ian should have a real room. The back and forth discussion felt endless to Alice until she finally pointed up the stairs and said, "Go! Please, go!"

Now that they have, she turns to Ian with a sigh of relief, scowling and inclining her head in the direction of the stairs. She mutters, "God—can you be polite to a fault?" and Ian says, "I know," and reflects her exasperated smile. Together they make up the sofa, unfurling sheets, tucking corners, plumping pillows, their movements familiar and fluid.

"There," Alice sighs.

Ian pats the sofa cushions.

"I'd forgotten how comfy this is," he says, and his eyes roam the room in a hungry way that sends an electric pulse shimmying up Alice's spine. "I'll need pajamas, Ally. I think there's an old pair up on the top shelf of our closet that I'll just run up and—"

"No. I gave that stuff away ages ago. I can probably dig up some of Ned's camping long-johns."

She has to plunge elbow-deep into cardboard boxes in the upstairs hall closet, through piles of old soccer cleats, netting, ice skates, a musty-smelling tent, a sleeping bag sprouting splotches of black mold. Twenty years of raising boys distilled into one spare closet. Clutching cold thermal underwear, she pads down the unlit stairs into the orange radiance of the living room and like a physical blow feels regret explode beneath her ribs at the tableau which greets her: Ian on the sofa in a circle of lamp glow, half-glasses clinging to the tip of his nose, reading *The New Yorker* with Rex curled at his side. The dog's tawny head in Ian's lap. Ian's delicate fingers absently stroking the short fur while the dog closes his eyes in bliss. Ian the scholar, the gentle soul, the father.

The man he might have been.

He looks up and catches her expression, smiles, and pats the sofa beside him.

"Come visit awhile. The kids are asleep." He winks. "Just like old times."

She remains standing. "I have to teach in the morning."

"The schools have no power."

"They might in the morning. I have to be prepared."

"Aw, third-graders. How much preparation can you need?"

She glares. He continues, now smiling in a way she thinks might be a smirk, "C'mon Ally. You're so smart, you can probably ad-lib the whole year's curriculum."

She examines the floor, lips pressed together, heat rising into her throat. "I—"

"See what I'm drinking?" He shakes the empty bottle. She reluctantly raises her eyes, face still inclined downward.

"I'm glad."

"Three months. Got the *chip,* going to the *meetings.*" His voice is a sing-song of disdain. How he used to argue with her about twelve-step programs!

"I'm glad. I really am." She pictures the Vespa among the old bicycles in her garage. "I guess losing your license was a wake-up call."

The corners of his mouth turn down.

"Nah. Nothing to do with that. I always said I'd do it when I was good and ready."

"You've been good and ready before. What—three times? Five?"

She hears the hardness creeping into her voice, the edge into his. He sighs, rubs his mouth.

"Ally, this time is different."

The skin on the back of her neck goosebumps at the words she's heard so many times before. At the same time her heart lurches dangerously.

"Can't you tell?" he murmurs. Her back muscles spasm. Oh, those armloads of wood she lugged up the stairs, the fire she kept going. How cold, how utterly empty it had been. How her lovely space fought her during the power outage: the cathedral ceilings, the open floor plan she and Ian had designed. All those empty bedrooms. Square footage that sucked the heat out of a room as fast as she labored to warm it.

"Ally?" Ian rises and touches her sleeve. His touch is feather-light. He closes his fingers gently around her arm, and she imagines the heat of his legs against hers in her bed, the weight of his pelvis draped against her hips.

"You've gotten strong," he says, releasing his grip and then stroking her biceps with the backs of his fingers. "Working out?"

She snorts. "Yeah . . . raking leaves, mowing the lawn, hauling those recycling bins to the curb every Wednesday . . ."

"You don't have to, you know," he says, still stroking her. "You never had to. You chose to make things—"

She stiffens, but her blood still tingles. "Good night, Ian." Her arm, drawing away, feels heavy as cement. The stairs rise like cliffs. She keeps her eyes forward, staring into blinding darkness, avoiding the photographs that line the staircase wall. Why see herself with Ian at their wedding, Ian and baby Ned two years later, Ian and the two babies a year after that? Why awaken the voice that whispers, *Why don't you just take him back, take him back, people can change.*

Alice spends the next day away from her house. The power remains out at school, but she picks up her materials from her office and plugs her computer into a socket at the coffee shop on Franklin Street. She is introducing a new unit on the history of Chapel Hill, and she downloaded a treasure trove of information the day before the storm. Now she has to cull through it for the most vivid, relevant bits. She takes a sip of latte, licks the froth off her lips, and dives into the work. The next time she lifts the cup to her mouth, the coffee is cold. She pauses, smiles. She doesn't look up again until she prickles with the sensation of being watched, and, lifting her eyes, sees her friend Luisa, the English as a Second Language teacher, holding a tray of food. "Talk about devoted!" Luisa says.

"I'm having fun," Alice replies, grinning. It is nearly noon, but when Alice snaps her computer shut and joins Luisa and another friend for sandwiches and hot coffee, she feels fresh, energized, as if she's just awoken.

Her health club has power, so in the afternoon she jogs around the indoor track. She runs into Nancy from her book club, and declines an invitation to dinner and a movie. Heading toward the locker rooms, she sees Nick Thompson, who teaches special ed and who is her closest friend at work. "Boy—everyone who's anyone is here!" she says, smiling. He offers to come install a generator for her. She feels less tongue-tied than she sometimes does talking to him at school, forgets she's sweaty and that her hair is matted to her head, even lays her hand on his arm in thanks when he offers to shovel her driveway the next day. She surprises herself by curling her arm to flex her muscles and saying, "Thanks, Nick, but I've got that all under control." He laughs.

"Well then, can I take you out for a nice, warm dinner tonight?"

"Ah—tonight—I can't. But—Friday night?"

He nods, and as they settle on a place and time she catches herself watching his lips, which look honest somehow, soft and wide in the midst of a cleanly shaven face.

She hums while waiting for a shower, until the fragments of conversation around her coalesce and she understands she's the only one there with heat and hot water. Her towels at home are thick and oversized; she's installed a pulsing, wide-diameter showerhead. Still, she keeps her place in line, waits the thirty-five minutes it takes to reach the shower stall with its narrow, lukewarm beam of water. She doesn't want to reach home too early.

And yet, pulling into her driveway at dusk, she is suffused with warmth. Every window in the house is a square of orange light, the door is unlocked, and an aroma of dill and garlic greets her. She's become so accustomed to coming home in darkness, fitting her key into the lock by feel, tripping over Rex as she flicks on the kitchen lights. Now Rex's ears perk forward and he lifts and drops his tail a couple of times but doesn't abandon his spot by the fire. Ian has probably walked him. The mail is stacked on the counter. The table, cleared of the clutter of magazines and week-old newspapers which Alice had merely pushed to one side the previous night, is set for six, with cloth napkins, with ice cubes melting in the water glasses. Ian was always the neater of the two. He is lounging on the couch, feet up, reading a theology book. Three other books are stacked by his ankles.

"The Romanians insisted on cooking dinner tonight," Ian says. "Stuffed zucchini. Did you know they live in one room?"

She peels off her gloves. "I told you—that basement apartment of Letty's. The former au pair's room."

"One bathroom, a hot-plate for cooking—for four people."

"Well, maybe that's what they're used to. Letty said they extended their lease."

"Aurica's a doctor."

Alice turns her back to the sofa and holds her palms out to the fire. He is trying to tell her something, impart some lesson like he used to do, but she isn't one of his undergraduates. The joy she felt at a day well spent is seeping out of her, leaving a residue of fatigue.

"Did you know that? That Aurica's a doctor?"

He's sitting in her favorite spot on the sofa.

"No, I didn't." She wants a glass of wine, but doesn't dare fetch a bottle from her pantry. "So, is your power still out? Did you check?"

"She can't practice in the States, of course," Ian continues. "They won't recognize her degree. But she said it doesn't matter to her—she needs to take care of her boys, her husband. It's all for the boys."

Alice sighs, shrugs. "Of course."

"What do you mean, of course?"

At the brittle, argumentative edge to his voice Alice turns and inspects him. His cheeks are flushed. She involuntarily sniffs the air. She squints at the empty O'Doul's on the coffee table, trying to tell if it's new or a decoy. Then she bites her lip. It is no longer your concern, she tells herself. "I mean, of course, that's why people become refugees, generally. For their children. For a shot at improving their lives."

The stairs creak and Alice smoothes back her hair. The Trandafir boys spill into the family room, followed by Aurica, her bleached hair twisted into a thin bun, and Simon, in a white button-down shirt and a tie. Rex gives one loud bark, jumps to his feet, and gives chase to the boys, who squeal and fly into the kitchen. On the tile island in the kitchen's center, a pitcher of lemonade rattles. Simon and Aurica both call "*Lee-neesh-teh*!" to the boys, but Alice says, "Oh—they're fine, let them have some fun!"

"I also discovered 'Trandafir' means 'rose,'" Ian says to Alice in the tone he uses with his students.

"Does it? How pretty."

"Is a changed name, made up," Aurica says flatly with a wave of her hand.

"Made up?"

Simon and Aurica exchange glances.

"Is not important. We make special dish for you to try—"

"Did you change it coming to the States?" Ian asks, while Alice's pulse gallops. She sees Aurica's neck flush.

"No, no," Simon stammers. His mouth twitches furiously. He takes a breath. "Is not important. In my father's time, was common, this, to change names. Not important."

"Fascinating," Ian says. "So—did people change their names to—assimilate? Or to hide religious differences . . . ?"

Simon shrugs and draws his open palm through the air as if clearing a slate. "Eh . . . not interesting, same story everywhere."

Alice thinks of the news stories she flips through on the nightly news, the streams of gaunt refugees crowding onto boats or into makeshift tents, fleeing brutalities she doesn't like to consider. But isn't that usually in Rwanda, or Bosnia, or Chechnya . . . ? Aurica's lips pale. Simon's twitch has spread from his mouth to his eye. Alice tries to catch Ian's attention. He presses ahead, "No, I'm interested. Was it for political gain . . . or religious . . ."

"OK—religion," Simon says as if conceding a point. "Nothing."

"Well, I study this, I'm an expert on religious persecution in Eastern Europe. So do you mean, were you Jewish, or part of a minority Christian sect that—"

"My father was Jewish, then Communist. So many names were changed during the war. Of course it made no difference when the legionnaires burst down your door." He stops abruptly, skidding on his own words. When he speaks again his voice is quieter. "I bore you. I am scientist, like I said. So, atheist. Here, we all become Americans. Finished. Let's talk other things." Simon rubs his palms together as if brushing crumbs off them, but his lips have thinned and his eyes burn.

"We are so lucky," Aurica says.

"Hear that?" Ian says to Alice, who frowns. "*Lucky.* They live

American Dreaming

....

112

in . . . close quarters, she had to give up her career, and yet, they feel lucky."

"We *are* lucky," Aurica repeats, eyebrows raised, face earnest like a child's.

Alice has pressed her lips together so hard that they feel numb. "It smells so delicious in here! Why don't we all sit down, and thank you so much for doing all this . . ."

"Please, is nothing," Aurica says, "the boys helped and Mr. Ian, of course, he do so much too."

To Ian, Alice says, "You didn't work today?"

"I went and retrieved my books, worked here. I like it here. Learned something new—how to make stuffed zucchini. Plus, four phrases in Romanian. Taught the kids about Buddhism. Boys— *remember?* The whole world is a school, not just the classroom, if you only let yourself look."

"Is true," Aurica says, a little stiffly, "but first is good get college diploma."

Their laughter fades under the scraping of chairs as they squeeze around the table. Alice glances nervously at Ian, and sure enough, his lips are pursed and she can tell he's composing a comeback.

"Not everyone is cut out for college," he says, his tone casual, as if he and Alice have not had this argument twenty times before. Alice catches Aurica's alarmed glance toward her sons, but Ian keeps going. "Our younger son, for example. There isn't much college could teach *him,* since he wants to be an actor. Sharp as a whip—could've been an investment banker if he wanted to. Or chair of a department. He's off in Hollywood now, good-looking kid, *tons* of talent. He'll be richer than us all in a couple of years."

Ian's mention of Danny is like a dentist's probe into a rotting tooth for Alice. He knows that she and Danny haven't spoken since the summer. He knows she doesn't agree with his decision to skip school in order to model. Party. She blames Ian for Danny's attitude: Ian's emphasis on cool. The way Ian used to turn on MTV with the boys; his Banana Republic clothes and constant borrowing of Danny's vintage shirts. Ian's college-student inflections, his sentences turning up at the end. And yet, hadn't she watched his antics in silence? Hadn't Alice also enjoyed having a hip husband?

Aurica's eyes dart to Alice and then swoop beyond, over Alice's left shoulder, fixing something beyond, her gaze so steady that Alice turns her own head. But there's nothing behind her except the large picture window, and through that, nothing. The other side of the street is black as obsidian. Then it dawns on Alice: Aurica is searching for a glimmer of light behind the curtains of their rented apartment, some sign that they are free to go.

Alice kicks Ian's shin under the table and says, "But college is a great idea for smart boys like you two!"

"I maybe become big rock star," the older boy says. "Like Eminem. Or Backstreet Boys. Is how you get rich in America."

"Three months, already—*specialist,* knows everything," Simon says with a nervous laugh.

The younger boy says, "I become big doctor like Mama." Aurica's pupils dilate and she smiles and strokes his cheek.

"It—it must be very hard for you, not being able to work," Alice says.

"I hope, soon, I do work," she answers, looking down at her plate. She pushes around the peeled pale green zucchini, plumped with meat and rice, that float in a sea of tomato sauce. She takes a breath, swings her face back up. "In fact, if Professor Ian knows of any position—secretary, assistant, anything—I am so thankful."

"But you're a trained doctor—" Alice says.

"They have plenty cardiologists already at Duke," Simon says, again in the jocose tone he seems to be trying on, like a suit of clothes. "As doctor *there,*" he jerks his head back, as if Romania lies over his right shoulder, "she wins—*earns*—one, two hundred. A month. Secretary here earn how much? So, you see. She wants something small, keep her mind occupied while the boys are in school, win some money, maybe we find small apartment we can buy."

Alice looks at Ian. Is he also thinking, two three-bedroom houses between the two of them? So much excess, so much squandering.

Ian rubs his mustache and squints at Aurica.

"You just help me as we discussed earlier . . ." His voice drops and Aurica nods, ". . . and I'll do my best. There are a ton of jobs in my department."

"That can't possibly be what you *want,* Aurica," Alice says, stumbling over the pronunciation of her name and wondering what the hell Ian is talking about.

"What I *want?*" Aurica looks confused. She chews her bottom lip and meets Alice's eyes. "A family do what they can one for another, isn't it?" Her direct gaze falters, then flits wildly around the room for a moment, settling onto her boys, slowing and certain, the way a bird eases onto its nest of eggs. Alice finds her own gaze wandering and discovers only Ian squarely watching her, eyes dark and questioning.

The following evening as they are setting the dinner table, the lights abruptly blink on across the street. A shout goes up from the Trandafir boys, who rush to the windows and jump up and down, hugging one another and the dog.

"You're welcome to stay for dinner," Alice says as Simon steps into his boots.

"Ah—I must turn on heat, turn off lights, not put strain on electricity . . ."

"But it'll be freezing for a few hours. Turn everything on and have dinner here," Alice says. "I have a roast in the oven."

"You have been such help," Aurica says, her eyes on her husband's receding form. "You give us wonderful house, good food, wonderful talking together . . ."

"Alice doesn't know how good she has it," Ian says.

Aurica looks from Ian to Alice, and then at her two sons who are zipping up their parkas by the back door. She says something in Romanian, and they hang their heads and begin unzipping.

"I help with dinner, no?" Aurica says to Alice, but her eyes flick to Ian. Alice smiles and hopes her face doesn't betray the enormous relief she feels at Aurica's words. Ian volunteers to fetch Simon back.

"Maybe you should check to see if your power's back, too," Alice calls, but without turning around, Ian shouts back, "It's not!"

Dinner is swift and silent, despite Ian's attempts to engage the Trandafirs in talk of American politics, the educational system, or religion. In the end only Ian is talking, quoting the reviews of his latest book. Aurica helps Alice clear the table, but nearly drops a stack of plates.

"Mrs. Alice," she says in a shaky whisper when the two are in the kitchen. "I ask you, is not better if Mr. Ian stay here?"

"Excuse me?"

Aurica blanches and Alice finds herself transfixed by the rapid rise and fall of her chest. "I say, please excuse me, but Mr. Ian is good man, smart man, and—and for women, to be alone is so hard, is not right—"

Simon comes in carrying a stack of plates, and Aurica's eyes bulge. He shoots her a questioning look, and she dashes out. After that, Simon seems to be everywhere: guiding his wife into her coat, the boys into their boots, all while thanking Alice profusely. Within minutes the Trandafirs are receding in a huddle from Alice's house, clouds of their breath trailing like a scarf around them. She waves from her picture window, Rex beside her, his tail arched upward and his ears forward, dog brow furrowed.

"Did she talk to you?" Ian says behind her. Alice spins around. "Who?"

"Aurica. Did she say anything?"

Alice's heart quivers. Her mouth goes dry. *Now* what has Ian done? She recalls the first of those long-ago phone calls, the angry, frightened voice of the young graduate student, Alice's own numbness, the all-enfolding stillness at the girl's confession. The girl's confidence that Ian meant what he'd said. It was the booze, Ian told her later, and later, and again. Always the booze. He thought Alice was smart enough to understand it meant nothing. Now she leans back against the window, folding her arms across her chest, and shakes her head.

Ian shrugs. "Oh well. I thought she would've said something to you. She seemed to agree with me." He turns back to the dishes. Alice frowns, her breathing returning to normal. This is different: Ian is referring to something he *wanted* Aurica to discuss with Alice, not something he fears she has. She joins him at the sink. The weight of warm wet plates against her fingertips feels good, and soon the silent rhythm of drying and stacking soothes her. Soap bubbles rise from the sink. She waits: Ian is a man who cannot tolerate silence.

"Aurica and I had a very interesting conversation about the human ability to—transform," he says, not thirty seconds later. "To completely re-invent oneself. Which I just wrote a paper about last month, so it's something I'm quite familiar with. Aurica believes in it whole-heartedly—how else would they have moved here?"

Alice tries to anticipate where this is going. Conversations with Ian can be mini-lectures. His right shoulder touches her left as he washes, warming her, and she doesn't move away.

"Aurica looked at her future in Romania and saw no future at all—for herself, without the right equipment or money, relying on bribes from her patients just to keep food on the table—or for her sons. Simon was perfectly happy in his job, but it was he who could get a visa to work *here*. So they stepped out of their lives—each one of them, Alice—they put behind them all that had happened before, all they'd been, and each changed, transformed. To help the others."

"So?"

"*So,* Aurica believes in *my* ability to transform, too. She was supposed to tell you. She seemed unfazed by the mistakes I've made in my life."

Alice's body sways slightly. She puts down the dishrag.

"You talked to her about . . . us? About what happened between the two of us? I think it's time for me to get to bed." Ian glances at his watch, and she does too.

"It's eight o'clock," he says, putting a wet hand on her blue cotton sleeve. Beads of water flatten into a dark imprint. "Aurica understood—why can't you? Maybe it's because she's European—but she *gets* it was always you I wanted to be with. To grow old with. You seemed to understand that for a long time, and then . . . I don't know."

"I'm not sure I ever understood about the other—"

He whispers, "You know, Alice, every *week* I meet a new woman, some beautiful new grad student or faculty wife, someone at a reading who wants me to go for coffee, and still it's *you* I want. That should mean *something* to you."

Alice can't block the heady rush of pride, of triumph, of belief. She stammers, "Ian, I—" but he holds up a hand. In the gesture she sees Ian as the graduate student she first met, holding up a hand against her objections to their dating, and then to their moving to North Carolina even though Alice was still years away from finishing her own degree. She had to learn to prioritize, he'd told her then. And hadn't she prioritized beautifully? She put aside her teaching ambitions, her friends, her doubts. She wasn't that different from Aurica, after all. At the thought of Aurica, a seed of worry pricks her mind. Ian's words now reach her as from a distance.

"It's been so lucky, the way my lack of power threw us back together, or perhaps it was pre-ordained, Alice. Sometimes we have to pay attention to omens. Aurica, a doctor, fully believes in omens."

"Did you bribe Aurica with the offer of a job?" Alice cuts in.

There is a beat of silence.

"What?" Ian blinks.

"A job, in exchange for talking me into—into—"

"For heavens sake, you think I need to *bribe* women to convince them of something?" Ian looks amused and incredulous. An idea begins to take shape in Alice's mind.

"You swear you didn't?"

"Look, this is unimportant next to what I'm talking to you about!"

"O.K. then, come with me." Alice grabs Ian by the wrist. A fine trembling has started in her middle and spread throughout her body, but she also feels awake, full of energy and a need to confirm one thing—any one thing she can. Ian laughs and says, "O.K., O.K., slow down . . ." but allows her to drag him out the door, no jacket. He catches her when her traction-less slippers skid on a patch of ice, and as she falls against his chest, she loses her momentum. She considers turning back into the house and steering him up to her room, forgetting her doubts, unplugging the phone and starting over. But they've arrived at her dented Ford Taurus, the car they'd intended to give Danny, and she remembers the gold Audi she let Ian keep, now with her son in California. "C'mon," she says more roughly than she intended, and soon they're zigzagging up her drive.

"Where are we going?" Ian asks, draping his arm over the back of her seat.

"You'll see." For a moment she is unsure herself.

As they pass Letty's house the lights behind the curtains in the basement send a stab of longing through her. She hits the gas and keeps driving, making a slow loop past the dark library, the grocery store, the school where she works.

"Eighty-nine people were treated for carbon monoxide poisoning at Duke, after the storm," Ian says. "A few died. We're lucky."

Even in Chapel Hill, in the warm, polite South, storms descend out of nowhere and destroy people's lives: that is Ian's point.

"The world is full of calamity," she says, but keeps to herself her next thought: here she is exactly where she'd most feared, alone, a loose thread, no longer woven into the fabric of familyhood. Her hands are numb against the icy steering wheel. Traffic signals are still down and her pulse jumps in her throat as she slows, then inches through each intersection. During their marriage, Ian would be the one to drive on nights like this. The car goes into a skid and she quickly turns the steering wheel as she's been taught, instead of in the direction she intuitively wants to spin it. The tires find solid ground again; she wordlessly thanks God.

"Good girl," Ian says. "Quite the all-weather driver now."

"Yup." Her heart shrinks to a knot within her chest. If Ian's changed, if he *has,* am I being an idiot? she thinks. Her mind drifts to the Trandafirs and sacrifice, of shedding a career, a language, the country of your birth. Forgiving someone a few years of indiscretion is just a drop in the sacrifice bucket compared to that. *That* is the moral of the story Ian tried to tell her earlier.

She feels Ian shift in the seat beside her as they enter his neighborhood. It's an older, more crowded neighborhood of smaller bungalows close to the UNC dorms. She rolls down her fogged windows to see better. The hum of emergency generators and the smell of wood smoke drift in.

"Ally, what's the point of this . . . ?" Ian says softly as they reach his block. She swerves around two orange cones connected by yellow police tape, cordoning enormous oak branches heaped right in the middle of the road.

"Alice," she snaps, "it's *Alice.*" As she suspected, the street is limned with lights. Even in Ian's dark bungalow, a golden glow shimmers behind a second-floor window. He always forgets and leaves the bathroom light on.

Her pulse steadies.

"O.K., *Alice,* what's—"

"Ian, you scoundrel," she says aloud, shaking her head, but suddenly it seems funny. The fist in her chest releases, and she smiles. "You are funny."

"*Funny?* So my power's back on; so?" Ian turns his body toward her, away from his house. It's as if he's trying to block the window with his bulk. He reaches for her cheek with outspread fingers. "It doesn't change what I was saying—"

"Yes it does." She ducks her face out of his reach. Her body is warming, despite the biting night air rolling through the windows. She makes a U-turn right over a patch of ice, and parks in front of his house. "It changes everything. You in my house is no omen. It's not chance, even if it was the first day, which I now doubt."

"Alice. Is it so wrong to take advantage of a situation that comes up, because I want us to be together again? That I—perhaps I—did a little engineering so we could—but only because without you I'm—I'm—"

"Please." Alice holds up her hand, then touches a finger to Ian's warm lips to stop him talking. His voice is becoming hollow and it tears at her. Her smile has faded, and she feels a new tenderness along with new resolve. "Ian, it's time for you to go home—*your* home," she says, her voice gentle but steady even though the trembling in her middle is back. "It turns out I *do* believe in a person's power to transform, Ian, just like Aurica does."

He frowns. "Well then, why are we playing these stupid games, driving all over hell and—"

"Please let me finish." She swallows and momentarily closes her eyes. When she looks up again, her eyelids are moist. "I believe in transformation, Ian, because it's happened to *me,*" she whispers.

He snorts and shakes his head in disbelief. He opens his mouth, pauses, then, to her surprise, closes it. She waits. The car is humid with their breath. He lifts his palms in the air; drops them.

"So all *I've* done—the O'Douls, the changing, you don't care?"

"I care that it's good for *you.*" She pauses. "I'll come get you in the morning, so you can pick up your motorbike." She waits. He lumbers out of the car, leans back in through the open window. His fine cheekbones, his velvet eyes are visible even in the semi-darkness.

"You're making a mistake," he says, his voice low, angry now.

"I may be." She waits. He pats himself down, extracting his keys from his breast pocket. He shakes his head again, then with a *pffff!* of disappointment turns away from the car. She waits until she sees the lights flick on in his house before pulling away. She drives slowly at first, waiting for the loneliness to descend. But with each block, she picks up a little speed, and as she pulls into her driveway she is dazzled by the light pouring from her kitchen windows.

Attempt, Unsuccessful

*E*liza Williams doesn't see him immediately, because as she hurries toward her office she is flicking at a patch of dried spit-up on her left shoulder. Just this morning she unwrapped her jacket from its dry-cleaning film, and here it is already blotched with baby formula. She sighs as the last white flecks flutter to the floor, and it is then that she notices the student slumped on the oak bench outside her office door.

She glances at her watch, unlocks her door and softly says, "Jeremy?"

No movement from the bench. She pauses, head cocked. Sighs. She walks into her office, flips on her desk lamp, sets down her briefcase. Pauses before hitting "restart" on the computer, closing her eyes and standing in the silence and utter stillness of the room. Her one noiseless hour, squeezed between drop-off at daycare and the endless stream of student voices, computer pings, telephone calls. She fights the urge to close her door and ignore the student asleep outside her office. But there's never been a student asleep there before.

In the hall she raises her voice. "Jeremy?"

The name bounces off the silent walls, back at her. She shivers.

"Jeremy!" she says again, her voice shrill, this time shaking him a little. "Jeremy! Jeremy!" His shoulder is warm. He moans. His head rolls forward, his eyes fly open, and he says, "Oh my God!"

Eliza takes a deep breath. Blows it out, then folds her arms across her chest, starting to smile. "Ah—silly me. I thought . . ." She shudders. "So, how long have you been—" but she's arrested by the tears in his eyes. "What is it?" she asks.

"I didn't think I'd ever wake up again," he says, and his face colors and he covers it with his hands.

Five minutes later he is sprawled on the small sofa in her office and Eliza has the phone to her ear. Between them, on her desk, is the small brown plastic medicine bottle, empty. The emergency room physician tells Eliza that the dose Jeremy took is not lethal, but that he'll be sleepy for a while longer.

"Did he take anything else?" the doctor asks Eliza, who repeats the question. Jeremy slowly shakes his head. He reaches into his navy backpack and pulls out two other bottles, rattling them like maracas. Eliza scans the labels and says into the phone, "He's got some Motrin and some Tylenol with him, but looks like they're mostly full—wait—yes, the Tylenol still has the store seal across the top."

The doctor tells her that a bottle of one of the other two might have killed him. Eliza shudders. On her sofa, Jeremy pulls his legs up under him and hugs his knees.

Hanging up the phone Eliza says, "Maybe we should walk over to the hospital."

"I am so, so sorry, Professor Williams," Jeremy says, squeezing his eyes shut as if in pain. His fair skin is so flushed that his blond eyebrows have nearly disappeared. "I didn't mean to put you through this—it's so stupid—"

"No—it's nothing to apologize about," she says. She thinks, *if it hadn't been my turn to drop Olivia at the daycare I wouldn't have been the first in the office this morning.* "But I do think you need to—see someone. A professional."

"I don't. Really. I'm fine. I just feel so—stupid. I don't know what I was thinking."

Eliza clears her throat. "What do you think you were thinking? I mean, were you trying to—you know, do yourself in?" Her voice drops with the last phrase, as if she'd uttered an obscenity.

Jeremy studies the top of his sneaker, picking at the lace.

"I have no idea."

"You have no idea?"

"Nope."

"Do you have a—a *theory?*"

Eliza's round gray eyes study him. Her raised eyebrows are almost hidden in the dark fringe of curls across her forehead. She props her chin with her thumbs and leans her elbows on her desk. She waits.

"It makes no sense," Jeremy finally says, meeting her eyes briefly and then looking down. "Everything's been going well lately, really. The best it's ever gone in my whole life. Why would I want to kill myself? It's insane. I—I'd just come by to ask you if I could have an extension on the final paper, but you'd gone for the day—it was, like, seven or something." He shrugs. She thinks, *at seven I was sit-*

ting next to the high chair feeding Olivia a jar of butternut squash. Olivia's round, chubby face flashes into Eliza's mind: the downy brown hair just appearing above her forehead, her enormous, glimmering brown eyes. Her warm-vanilla milky breath. A surge of warmth shoots through Eliza's chest. She thinks, this tall, muscular sophomore with a week's worth of razor stubble on his cheek was someone's own sweet baby once.

"Maybe we should call your parents?"

"No!" Jeremy springs to his feet, palms out, shaking his head.

"I just thought—so they can help."

"No. Really. Please. Believe me, it would make things much, much worse for me if you call them. My mother—oh, you couldn't *begin* to understand. It would be the last straw. Please, Professor Williams."

His blue eyes are pinned on hers, and he's clasped his hands together as if in prayer. He's been in her office twice before: to discuss his paper on Virginia Woolf, and to go over course requirements for a junior seminar. In class he is mostly silent. He turns his work in on time. She thinks of his poor mother, getting news like this; of any mother finding out her child, the joy of her life, tried to self-destruct. She sighs.

"The counseling center, then? Shall I call them for you?"

"I—I don't think I'll need that. God—I'm so sorry to take up your time like this. I know you're really busy. I'll just go back to my room now, and see you later in class. O.K.? Really. Everything is just fine. Perfect." He sweeps the Motrin and Tylenol bottles toward his backpack but Eliza catches his wrist.

"So perfect you're guzzling pills?" she says before she can stop herself. His eyes fill again and he chews his bottom lip and looks at the floor. He releases the medicine bottles onto her desk, and one falls on its side and rolls in a semicircle. He drops back onto her couch.

"I—I wasn't thinking. I didn't mean for you to find me. Look—it's not your shit—excuse me, it's not your problem to deal with and I apologize. Just—don't get my parents involved in all this. They don't need it. They mean well, they really try, but they're—different. I'll call the counseling center, O.K.?"

"Good."

"O.K." She wonders about her legal obligation to disclose something like this to the dean, to Jeremy's parents. In graduate school, only two years behind her, she learned to write, to teach, and to read texts critically. Not to read *students,* which she now thinks would have been infinitely more useful.

"O.K.," he mutters again, to himself. He doesn't move from her sofa. She glances at the clock on her screensaver.

"Anything—anything you want to talk about?" she says. He shakes his head, not looking at her. Why did he show up in *her* office? She touches her recently-cut hair, which has made her look much more matronly than she intended, especially coupled with the weight she hasn't managed to lose since having Olivia. She clears her throat. "Are you—are you enjoying the class?" she asks, and then flushes. I was making small talk with a suicidal student, she pictures herself telling her husband at dinner.

Jeremy nods his head.

"Will you take Lit 301 with me in the fall?" *You idiot,* she tells herself.

But instead of the incredulous snarl she expects to see on his face, tears well up in Jeremy's eyes for a third time, spilling onto his cheek when he gives a curt shake of his head.

"Won't be here in the fall," he says, but as her jaw drops he quickly adds, "I don't mean it like *that*. I'm transferring in the fall, that's all. Nothing dramatic. Have to." He forces a smile. "No big deal, though. I've had a good run."

"Oh!" she says. Her tone of voice says, *aha!*

"That's *not* why." There is a note of impatience in his voice. He erases it with his next sentence, sounding calm, even pleased. "I'm happy to transfer to State. I mean, I've loved it here, but it's too much for my parents. Having a *Dukie* in the family . . . beyond their wildest dreams! They need a break. And I'm used to moving, changing gears. Done it all my life. Look—last night was just a stupid, twenty-year-old thing to do. I bet it happens every day on campus. I'll walk over to the counseling center right now, if that'll make you feel better. But let's both forget this ever happened, O.K.?" He stands, and this time moves toward the door.

"O.K.," Eliza says. He pauses, and then out of his backpack he brings out a manuscript.

"The final paper," he says, setting it on her desk.

"I thought you needed an extension?"

"Nah. I get *your* papers done on time." He flashes a smile and is gone.

The moment he is out of the room Eliza's fingers tap her keyboard, searching her online data base for Jeremy's parents' phone number. As she copies it onto a Post-It, the telephone rings. It's the daycare: Olivia has pink-eye and must be taken home.

"But her eyes looked perfectly fine this morning, and I have a class to teach in an hour!" There is a silence, in which Eliza can picture the woman on the phone shrugging. "Have you—have you called my husband? He works at home, it's easier for him to—"

"There was no answer there."

"O.K., give me twenty minutes." Eliza presses the Post-It with Jeremy's parents' number onto her date book, intending to call from her cell phone in the car, but first she has to arrange with her teaching assistant to take over the class she'll miss that morning, and then there's traffic, and then she's holding her baby who is fussing and whose right eye is red and oozy and she forgets all about Jeremy.

It isn't until Eliza is sitting in the crowded waiting room at the pediatrician's and her cell phone rings that she thinks with a pang, *I have to call Jeremy's parents.* It's her husband on the phone.

"There was a message from the daycare—"

"She has pink-eye. I'm at the doctor's, just to make sure."

"I can meet you there. If you need to get back in to work—"

"She seems uncomfortable, so I want to hear what the doctor says. You can relieve me after. Hey—I had a student come in this morning who tried to overdose on some pills last night. I'm thinking of calling his mother."

She hears the exclamation of surprise on the other end, and adds that she sent him for counseling.

"Well, then. That's taken care of."

"Why would someone *do* something like that?" she asks. "I'm gonna call his parents. Just for my own peace of mind. I want to *understand.*"

But Olivia is squirming in her lap, batting the phone away from her mouth. It's not until she's back in her kitchen near noon, after delivering Olivia into her husband's arms, that she can make the call.

The woman answers the phone, "Yeah?" In the background, a television competes with a jack-hammer-like noise. Eliza watches her husband blow raspberries against their baby's round stomach until the little girl shrieks with pleasure. Their kitchen table is stacked with bills, unread issues of *The New Yorker,* and manila folders containing work her husband has brought home. The pile is crowned with a rattle and a teething ring.

"Is this Mrs. Dana Stallings?' Eliza asks.

"We don't want any." The line goes dead. Eliza frowns for a moment at the receiver in her hand, and then hits redial.

"Mrs. Stallings, I'm Professor Williams, one of Jeremy's teachers at Duke—" she says, speaking as quickly as she can. "I don't blame you, those pesky telemarketers always call around mealtimes—" and she pauses, giving Jeremy's mother an opportunity to apologize. The line is silent except for a drawn-out sigh. Then a weary voice says, "O.K., now what's he done?"

"Done? He—he hasn't done anything—no, I'm calling because I'm concerned about him—I thought you and I should talk about a few things."

"Shoot."

"Excuse me?"

"Go on, then." The jack-hammer noise has stopped. A child wails in the background, and Eliza hears the woman snap, "God's sake, Christopher, you set that thing down! Don't make me come over there! All right, then, go on." The woman's voice is gravelly and her thick Southern drawl makes Eliza think of Mississippi.

Eliza realizes the last phrase is directed at her, and she feels mute.

"Well? You were saying about Jeremy? You'd think time they get to college, they could take care of their own selves. 'Specially one that gets to Duke, brainy all his life."

"Maybe—Mrs. Stallings, could you possibly drop by my office later today? Or in the morning? I'd rather talk about this face to face."

A long sigh. Eliza watches her husband sift through a basket of toys, selecting the most enticing ones for Olivia's playpen.

"Drive all the way to Durham? I'm not done with the laundry, or the groceries, and Christopher's running around butt-naked—I'm trying to train him, you know, and they say to leave his bottoms off but he's already pissed on the carpet twice today—look, if you got something to say, just say it and be done with it and I'll get my husband to deal with Jeremy when he's got time."

"You know, why don't I drive out to you?" Eliza hears herself saying. Her husband jerks his head toward her, frowning, raising his palms to the ceiling. She shrugs at him. More and more she's thinking she cannot over the phone tell a mother her son tried to kill himself, and more and more she thinks a mother would want to know. "Siler City, right? That won't take me more than forty-five minutes."

"Suit yourself," Dana says, and gives her directions.

Jeremy lies face-up on the grass in front of the Chapel, eyes closed, basking in the April sun. His head rests on his backpack. His thoughts are racing and he can't quite drift into sleep, and his skin is still prickled like goose flesh despite the heat. A shadow drifts between him and the sun and he opens one eye and squints up.

"Martin!"

He abruptly sits up.

"Where were you? I was worried."

"Have a seat!" Jeremy pats the grass.

"Where were you all night?" Martin remains standing.

His eyes run up and down Martin's thin frame, taking in the neatly pressed khaki shorts, the crossed arms, the frown.

"Don't worry, nowhere I shouldn't have been," Jeremy says with a smile.

"What the hell does that mean?" Martin shifts position and a beam of sunlight falls into Jeremy's eyes. He looks away and his smile fades.

"Nothing. I'm sorry. I fell asleep outside Williams' office, that's all."

"You didn't even tell me you were going out."

Jeremy shrugs, and Martin drops onto the grass beside him.

"Last thing I know, you're filling out those stupid roommate preference forms for State. You're bitching about how no one there will know about you and how you're—"

"Sshhh!"

"God's sake, there's no one here!"

"We're in front of the damn *Chapel*! It doesn't get more public than that!"

Martin rolls his eyes, shakes his head. Sighs.

"O.K. Point is, last thing I know, you're sitting at your desk, all down. We make plans for dinner, I go to my seminar, and you never show. I'm up half the night."

"Nice to know you care," Jeremy says, again with a smile.

"Oh, fuck you." Martin looks away.

Jeremy touches his arm, and leans toward Martin.

Attempt, Unsuccessful

....

133

"I did something really stupid last night, if you must know, and I thought I'd go into the Chapel and pray about it. But it's been a while since I've been in there, and I started to think, I have no right. I don't belong in there. Just like I don't really belong on this campus. I will probably fit in much better at State."

"That is bullshit and you know it," Martin says. "And what is it that you did last night?"

"That wasn't the point of my story."

"I think I have a right to know." Martin squints at Jeremy. Jeremy pulls some blades of grass up through his fingers. He shrugs and mumbles, "Don't—freak out or anything. I'm fine. I just—I—I—I overdosed on some stuff. Couldn't even get that right, though. Fell asleep, or maybe chickened out, halfway through, so I didn't take all the stuff I was gonna."

Martin's jaw drops.

"Shit, man—you didn't—"

"Yup."

Martin squeezes Jeremy's shoulder. Jeremy shrugs his hand off.

"I mean, are you all right? Do you need—"

Jeremy shakes his head. "I talked to Williams. She's a cool lady."

Martin says, "I know it's tough, the coming out crap. But you gotta weather it, man. You can't go taking pills and shit."

Jeremy lifts his eyes so that he finally meets Martin's. But now it is Martin who drops his gaze, frowning at the freshly mown grass.

Eliza matches the number on her Post-It to a number on a mobile home, then sits in her car, window down, looking at the small white building pushed up against the back of its lot, the chain link fence encircling it. Across the street where a convenience store is going up, earthmovers rumble over the torn red clay. Men in hardhats shout in Spanish. Eliza feels unsteady, disoriented, as if she is in a foreign country. She concentrates on the hot-pink azaleas blooming on either side of the house's front door. The yard is neatly mown, strewn with plastic toys. The screen door opens and a woman with bleached blonde hair twisted into a knot on her neck steps through. A half-naked toddler clings to her hip.

"Professor Williams?" the woman calls. "I'm Dana. Come on in, come in!" As Eliza gingerly steps into the yard, Dana shouts, "I gotta apologize for the way I sounded on the phone. It's just been such a hell of a morning."

Eliza follows the woman into a living room littered with toys and children's clothes. The woman scoops an armload of clean laundry out of an armchair, and motions for Eliza to sit.

"Sure appreciate your stopping by," Dana begins, releasing the toddler to the floor. He picks up a toy train, and hands it to Eliza, who smiles at him and takes the train. Dana offers her iced tea.

"I guess y'all at Duke must be as busy as I am, so it must be pretty important. So. What's up with Jeremy?"

Eliza clears her throat. She takes a small sip of iced tea and chokes on its cold sweetness.

"Excuse me," she says. Dana watches her with calm round blue eyes. "Mrs. Stallings—"

"Dana."

"Dana, has Jeremy had any problems lately, or seemed unhappy to you?"

"What's he got to be unhappy about? Smart, good-looking, gets into Duke—only one from his high school, y'know. Always been top of his class. Ain't too happy leaving Duke, I reckon, but he's had two years. With his father getting laid off—and we've got the other kids to think of too." She taps a cigarette out of a box on the coffee table, lights it and takes a long draw. The toddler runs his hands affectionately over the dark blank television screen between them. Eliza suppresses a cough.

"Well, I'm afraid Jeremy made a suicide attempt last night," Eliza says, rather more abruptly than she'd meant to.

"A—a *what?*" She slaps a palm to her cheek. "My Lord—but we spoke just—hey—Christopher, don't you *dare* yank on that TV cord or the whole thing will crash down on your head again!" Dana springs out of her chair and pulls the child away from the entertainment center. He begins to howl. A half-inch cylinder of ash trembles on the tip of Dana's cigarette, then falls to the carpet. She doesn't seem to notice as she sits back down. "You go on—I'm listening to you, too, Professor Williams—mothers have to do five things at once sometimes—*hush,* Christopher. Is Jeremy O.K.? *Hush,* baby." She bounces the child on her knee and wraps an arm around him, cooing into his long hair. She holds her cigarette high in the air, away from the boy. Eliza watches Dana with amazement. The news seems to have made just a small wrinkle in Dana's day.

"He—he took a bottle of pills . . ." Eliza says.

"Jeremy's fine, though?" Dana's voice cracks. Her pale eyebrows rise, wrinkling her forehead. "Right?"

"Well, I guess, but—" A buzzer sounds. Dana's eyes flick toward her kitchen, and she exhales.

"Thank goodness," she mumbles, momentarily closing her eyes.

She opens them and says, "The dryer's done." Eliza isn't sure if Dana means thank goodness her son is all right or thank goodness the laundry is dry. Settling Christopher into a new spot on the carpet, Dana surrounds the boy with plastic ducks, a train whistle, a stacking toy, and smiles down at him. He flashes her a wide grin in return.

"I love this age," Dana says, then sighs. Her eyes narrow into a tired expression. "They get older, the problems start and you wonder, what's the point? There's no controlling that boy, you know. Smartest of the bunch, but *different*. I've tried and tried with him. Thank *the Lord* my other four are more—oh, I don't know, ordinary everyday sort of children. I'm not faulting Jeremy—it's likely his daddy—my others have my second husband for a daddy. Now Jason, he's an even-tempered sort of man."

Dana sucks on her cigarette, frowns, and rises.

"Always restless to get somewhere else, that boy. Siler City didn't suit him, or Fayetteville, or Hickory before that. Couldn't *wait* to get to Duke, but that hasn't been the bed of roses he expected, neither. But he can't go swallowing a bunch of pills every time something doesn't go his way. Lord knows I tried with that child."

Eliza wonders about the etiquette of the situation. She thinks she should touch Dana's arm or shoulder, but Dana is pacing in circles around Christopher.

"I know this must be very upsetting to hear," Eliza says. "That's why I wanted to come in person, rather than tell you over the phone. I thought I could help—"

Dana stops pacing and drops her cigarette butt into her glass of tea. It hisses and goes out.

"Miz Williams, have you got children?"

"I—yes—a baby—"

"Well, enjoy that baby. Babies, toddlers—*umh*—" she squeezes Christopher's fat thigh affectionately— "then, it's all downhill from there."

"I just couldn't fathom it," Eliza tells her husband over dinner that evening. "God, I wish I could have a drink."

He holds out his beer. "A sip won't hurt."

"I don't want a sip. I want a whole gin and tonic, but I'm not about to have it while I'm nursing Olivia. That woman! Chain-smoking around a baby, too worn out to even care that her oldest son just tried to kill himself—and there I was, *sure* she'd want to get in the car with me and drive right back to Durham as soon as she heard! Now I know why poor Jeremy didn't want me to contact them. Just imagine having parents who don't give a damn."

"You don't know they don't give a damn—"

"Oh, but I do. If anything she seemed—*annoyed*—that I came out to give her the news. Poor Jeremy, getting stuck with a mother like that!"

Olivia whimpers. Eliza darts up from the table and lifts her out of the baby swing.

"Finish your dinner. She can wait a few minutes."

"Imagine if she ever did anything to try to hurt herself." She shivers and her shoulders rise involuntarily. "God, I'd be just devastated."

Thursday evening Jeremy is rolling aluminum kegs across the grass toward his frat house when he hears his name called.

"Yo—Stallings!" His frat brother waves a phone out the window. "Your dad!"

"My stepdad," Jeremy says under his breath, and rolls the keg faster into the entryway. He wipes his damp palms on his jeans, takes the phone, and closes the door of the kitchen.

"What's up, Jason?" he says.

"I'm calling to ask you that." Jeremy hears his stepfather clear his throat, sounding embarrassed. "Your mother wanted me to call."

"O.K."

"Your—ahem, teacher? Some lady professor? Came by to see your ma couple days ago."

Jeremy stiffens. He says nothing.

"Everything all right, son?"

"Yeah."

"You need any money?"

"Nah. You got a job yet, Jason?"

"I'm looking, son, I'm looking."

"Do—do *y'all* need any money?"

He hears Jason's throaty laugh, his voice thickened by years of smoking.

"We're managing, Jeremy. Don't worry about us. But your ma's real busy, with Christopher and then driving Laura around to sum-mer job interviews and the like, and the others, *you* know—and she was worried about you. I told her, nothing to worry about, Dana, Jeremy's got his head screwed on right. She says, I don't know about that."

Jeremy feels as if he's been punched in the gut. He has no breath with which to speak.

"You there, son?"

Jeremy nods.

"Jeremy?"

"Yup."

"Anyhow. She doesn't get into details with me, you know how she is. I told her, boys do stuff at twenty that they get over. They grow out of."

Jeremy nods.

"Son?"

Into Jeremy's mind flashes the image of his mother's face when he tried to tell her about him and Martin. He sees again the way the ridges encircling her eyes deepened as she narrowed her eyes, looking away from him, her hand trembling as she lit another cigarette. He hears again her slow response, her raspy voice, her eyes not meeting his as she said, "Whattya want for supper?"

Her reaction to the biggest news he'd ever had to tell her.

"You there, Jeremy?"

"Yeah."

"All right, then. You partying any this weekend?"

Jeremy snaps back into himself. Shakes his head.

"Yeah. My frat's having a big one tonight."

"All right. Be kind to the ladies."

"Always am."

"And study. Just cause you're leaving in a few weeks don't mean you gotta let the grades slide, hear?"

"Yup."

"Your mother sends her love."

"Yeah. Me too."

By the time Martin arrives at the semi-formal, Jeremy has had three plastic cups of lukewarm beer. His cheeks are flushed, and the borrowed tuxedo he wears pinches at his waist. His date, Melissa, has already downed two beers.

"I can't believe you brought a *girl,*" Martin hisses through his teeth into Jeremy's ear.

"I had to. Last big event of the year, next year I'm gone . . . anyway. Melissa's cool with being just friends. Look, she's already scanning the crowd for someone to pick up."

"So you're really not gonna come out to your brothers before—"

"Sshh! No, I'm not." He snaps the paisley cummerbund of Martin's tuxedo. "Spiffy."

Martin shrugs. "Got it last week. 'Last big event of the year.' My high school one's too tight."

He takes a little silver flask out of his breast pocket.

"Want some Johnnie Walker?" he asks Jeremy. "I'm not about to drink that pisswater," he adds, nodding at the keg.

Jeremy pushes the flask away.

"For us country folk, that pisswater's pretty darn good!" he says. "My stepfather would be in heaven around a keg of Bud!"

He refills his cup, high-fives a few of the guys who've just come in. Watches the stung expression on Martin's face. Manages a smile when Martin shakes his head and disappears into another room. Downs the beer, fills his cup, feels his ears burn. Unknots his bowtie. Leaves the din of the party and climbs to the second floor.

Eliza and her husband have just settled onto their sofa to watch a rerun of "Seinfeld" when the phone rings.

"Let the machine get it," her husband says.

"I don't want it to wake Olivia," she whispers, and lifts the receiver. She can barely understand the words the caller is saying above the blare of music, laughter, yells.

"Who is this?" she asks again.

She makes out the name, "Jeremy Stallings," and plugs her other ear, trying to understand. The voice on the other end is shouting, and Eliza picks out a note of panic. Then, quite clearly, "He's—he's half out a window and I can't get him back in."

"What?"

"I don't know what to do . . ."

"Where is he?"

Eliza scribbles the dorm name on the back of an envelope and glances at her watch.

"Tell him I'm coming, tell him hang in there," she says, then presses the "off" button. She sits holding the receiver as her husband asks what is going on. "You don't need to be going out this time of night," he says.

Eliza hesitates for another heartbeat, then punches 911 into the phone.

Martin tiptoes back up the stairs to the second-floor bedroom. The lights are off and the air is heavy with the smell of sweat and beer.

"Jeremy," he says. Jeremy has both legs over the window sill, his backside on a desk. He's holding a half-empty beer.

"Just go away, Martin." His words slur.

"I called Professor Williams."

"You *what*?!"

"She's coming."

"Why the fuck would you call one of my professors? What kind of a moron—"

"Jeremy, just calm down and come back in. She's coming. She said hang in there."

"Oh, *God*!"

"She seemed worried. You don't want her to get here and find you—*y'know*—"

"Poor Professor Williams! She's gonna think I'm crazy, after our *last* meeting . . . she's coming *here*? Now? You're right about one thing anyway, Marty boy. She's the only one who seems to give a shit about me, about most people she meets . . ."

"That's so untrue, Jeremy," Martin says. "You know I care about you." Even as he says this, Martin can't help taking a step backward, away from the gaping darkness in the window. From his new distance he can see out the windows beyond Jeremy's body: the Gothic lines, the lead-paned windows of the dormitories across the quad. Shouts and laughter waft up. "You know I'm always gonna be there for you," Martin says, taking another step backward. Jeremy shakes his head, drops it into his hands.

"I just needed some air. I don't understand why you had to call Professor Williams," he says, but Martin thinks he sees a slow smile play on Jeremy's lips.

Two plainclothes campus police officers enter the frat house, while three in uniform approach the window from the outside.

"Jeremy Stallings?" one asks, but students dart away from them. Some drop cups of beer onto the tables behind them. Beer spills and slowly seeps across the floor.

"What's going on?" a fraternity brother asks, and an officer flashes a badge. He starts up the stairs, a knot of students following.

"Is someone in trouble?" Melissa whispers, joining the officers as they climb the stairs and approach a closed door.

On the other side of the door Jeremy is saying to Martin, "I just don't want anyone other than Professor Williams to know about this. Promise?" Martin nods. Jeremy swings his other leg back into the room, and finds he is panting. His muscles are quivering as if he'd just finished a marathon. The door slams open. Jeremy is still seated on the window sill, but now his body is mostly inside the room rather than out.

Melissa gasps. Behind her, other students crane their necks, press against her, trying to see into the room.

The taller, stockier of the two police officers reaches Jeremy's side in two strides.

"Jeremy Stallings?" he says. As Jeremy nods, looking dazed, the officer snaps a cold metal handcuff on his wrist.

"What the—"

"Now stay calm, son—"

"Hey, you gotta read him his rights! I know all about Miranda and—"

"It's not like that," the officer says. "He's not being arrested. Now, clear a path, please."

Jeremy strains against the handcuffs.

"Then what about these?"

The officer pries him away from the window.

"What've I done? Where are you taking me?"

"We're here to help. From what Professor Williams told us, we need to get you to a hospital, son—"

"What!? I don't want—I was only fooling—I never meant—I was already on my way in—" Jeremy's words trip over one another and he starts to pant.

"It's not a bad idea to get help, Jeremy," Martin says. Jeremy looks wildly at the circle that has formed around him, his brothers, the dark eyes, the silent faces. The black tuxedos, the flash of sequins on strapless gowns, some people holding beer cups, others clutching their arms as if cold.

"Where's Williams? Is she here?" Jeremy says to Martin.

"All right. Come on, son."

"I'm not your damn son—"

"Come on. You'll be fine in no time."

"I didn't mean for him to end up in the hospital," Eliza says to her husband three days later, over dinner. "I don't know how his family will afford *that*—maybe I should have gone over myself, instead of sending cops."

"I don't think you need to be any more involved in all this than you already are," her husband says with a frown. "You're not his mother, you know. He has a mother."

"Yes, I know," she says. Her eyes wander over her husband's shoulder, out the window of their small house to where the magnolia blossoms are opening in the eighty-degree heat. "The dean keeps calling too—they want him to take a leave, not have this semester count, come back next. But Jeremy is resisting that. Easy for the dean, letting a semester not count—the money, of course, the *tuition* bill still counts." Eliza squints out the window, fork suspended in mid-air.

"Eliza?" her husband says gently. "Honey, your dinner's gonna go cold."

She shakes her head, puts her fork down and massages her temples.

"I just feel like he needs something—someone—I can't quite explain it. Like everything would be all right for him if he just had someone *there* for him." She thinks of the apartment she grew up in on Ninety-sixth Street in Manhattan, the shelves lined with books, her parents playing Scrabble after dinner at the glass table in the dining room. Her nose stings, and in that instant Olivia starts to cry and Eliza pushes back her chair.

"Give her a minute—finish your dinner, she'll settle down," her husband says, but she is up, she's there, she has already filled her arms with the sweet weight of her baby.

If Wishes Were Horses

*I*t happened so quickly that later all Robert could say was, "The wonder of it all is that people don't drive off the road more often." To the policemen in the emergency room he kept repeating, "I guess I was just more tired than I thought." They'd found no alcohol in his blood, and he didn't volunteer that he and Ora had been en route to Crook's Corner for drinks when the concrete barrier got in the way.

"Is it possible he dozed at the wheel, ma'am?" one of the cops asked Ora in the adjoining cubicle.

"I don't think so," Ora said. "We were having a conversation, clear as day, at the time." Her words came slowly, making her seem slightly dazed, but her brown eyes burned and her cheeks were flushed. As she perched on the edge of the gurney, with her slim legs swinging over the side and both hands gripping the edge, she quivered with energy. Her knuckles were white, as if it were only with effort that she was able to resist springing down.

"You were talking at the time," the policeman repeated, scribbling on a pad. "Do you remember what you were discussing?"

"Excuse me a moment." She laid a hand gently on the arm of the physician assistant who was sewing closed the long thin gash on the side of her face. With her other hand she smoothed down her hair. "Honey?" Her smile twisted into a momentary wince as her muscles pulled her skin open. "Honey, I do believe that anesthetic is wearing off. I think I can feel the little . . . needle pricks."

"I'm sorry," the physician assistant said. He refilled a small syringe and as he held it poised over Ora's cheek, she turned her smile to the policeman.

"Sir," she said. Her words stretched like molasses. "Perhaps we can do this another time? The anesthetic makes me just a bit drowsy and I find my speech gets a bit slurred."

They didn't talk in the taxi going back to Ora's apartment. She put a kettle on the stove and started running water in the tub. Robert followed her from the kitchen to the bathroom, keeping a few steps between them. In her bedroom she slid her mint-green dress over her head.

"God, I feel as if I've been run through a pepper mill," she said, invisible beneath the cloth. "Will you pull this thing off? My arm's too sore."

He did and then they were face to face.

"Don't stare at me like that," she said. "It's not becoming."

"We're lucky we weren't killed," he said.

"That's a matter of opinion." She found the flowered silk robe he'd given her for Valentine's day and walked stiffly toward the kitchen, where the kettle was already screaming.

"I think you need professional help," Robert said.

"Tea?"

"I mean it."

"I told you if you ever saw her again I would kill us both," Ora said. "You promised. You gave your word."

"I have no recollection of that," he said.

"Last November."

"I never said that. And anyway, she's twenty-six, for God's sake. I have a daughter older than that!"

"All the more reason for it to make my blood boil."

He opened the cupboard above the sink, frowned, closed it.

"Above the dishwasher," she said. "I told you yesterday."

"Right." He took out a mug that said *#1 Secretary*.

"That's the problem," she said. "I don't think you ever listen to me when I talk to you any more."

He grunted. "I didn't promise you not to ever see her again. How could I? She works right across the hall."

Ora squeezed her eyes shut. Her cut oozed a clear fluid. Her knuckles blanched around her teacup. She opened her eyes and blinked twice, then smiled a small pressed-lip smile.

"You told me she had left the company." Her voice was a whisper.

"I did?"

"In November. Last November. After our—never mind."

"Wait."

"Let go of my wrist."

"Ora, I swear I don't remember saying that. Maybe you're confusing Jennifer with someone else—"

"There are others?"

They were eye to eye again. She imagined how awful she must look: no makeup, stitches running up her face.

"There's been no one but you for the past three years," he said, and she stopped pulling the wrist he was still clutching and her body felt suddenly light.

"Not that you haven't had opportunities," she said.

"There are always opportunities."

"I just can't stand the thought of you with anyone else, Robert," she said. "I know it's crazy, but I can't. You say it's just dinner but how can I be sure? How can I know?"

She freed her wrist and brushed a strand of silvery hair out of his eyes.

"Come on, honey, let's drop the whole thing," he said. He kissed her lips lightly, and she pressed against him. She started to unbutton his shirt, unzip his pants. She bit his ear.

"Were you scared, out in the car?" she whispered. "Did you think it was the end?" She crushed his lips with hers and pulled him down toward the floor. He put his hands on her shoulders and locked his knees.

"I'm too sore," he said. "Come on. I'll take a bath with you. Let me just find a towel."

She let her robe slip to the floor and ran her fingers lightly down the curve of her neck. Her body was still small, firm. She would never be one of those women with sagging breasts; she was too small boned, too finely built. She was about to spring after him when she saw him open the door to the hall closet and close it, and then go into the bedroom. She heard more closet doors open and close. He called, "Honey, where do you keep those damned towels?" and her heart turned in her chest and her breath caught. He'd been with her in this apartment for nearly three years, since she'd had to give up her Victorian house and move into this cramped two-bedroom. He'd helped her unpack boxes and put up wallpaper and he'd bought the towels that were stacked in the bathroom cupboard where they'd always been and which he took out whenever he came over, hundreds of times.

From the public phone booth beside the ladies' room in the restaurant, Ora dialed her own number. Her answering machine picked up on the first ring, and she punched in her code and waited to hear her messages played back. The first two were from girls at work, and the third was from a man she'd nearly forgotten whose husky voice said, "Hey honey, it's been almost a year since we hooked up. Happy birthday baby! When can I see you again?"

The machine beeped three times and fell silent. She slammed down the receiver and then quickly glanced around, but the hall was empty. She headed back toward the table, wondering if her mother would start in on her again—the constant reminders that she was forty now and that this was a milestone, a birthday different from all the others.

There were five crabapple trees in the front yard alone, and this time of year they exploded into a fragrant cloud of white and pink and Ora never used to mind that they shaded out the sunlight from the living room. She would open her windows in the mornings and by dinnertime her wood floors would be carpeted with soft white petals. That image paraded through her mind now, as she made two tours around the block and finally parked across the street from her old house. The tenants were keeping her hedges neatly clipped.

In church last week she confessed that she had been lying to

Robert about having sold her house. Then she laughed and confessed that she'd been hiding this from the priest for the past three
years. Robert had been so insistent and she hated arguments. But
why should that woman win out, she asked the priest. Why should
that woman get to keep the big stone mansion next to Ora's house,
which she hadn't even bought, while Ora lost the only big investment
she had ever made? Why should Ora give up her house? She didn't
remember the priest's answer. She told him too that she, after all,
was the one who had been born in Chapel Hill and lived there her
whole life. That woman was from up North. Sooner or later she'd
want to go back where she belonged. After all, she'd only moved
down when Robert's company transferred him to North Carolina.
Why she stayed after Robert left her remained a mystery to Ora.
This, Ora didn't confess.

"She doesn't want to have to move the kids," Robert had said.
"They're all so settled in the schools here."

"But aren't all her relatives up in New York?" Ora asked.
"Wouldn't the kids be better off being near their grandparents and
all?"

"I'd like to see them every once in a while too, Ora."

Ora's eyes drifted from her magnificent crabapple trees to the
stone house next door, where the front door was swinging open and
now there *she* was. Holding a pair of pruning shears before her, step-
ping lightly, bouncing down the front steps, it seemed to Ora. Her
lips were rounded into an *O* and Ora squinted. Was she *whistling*?
She wore green pants which were speckled with dirt, and a big
red and black plaid shirt. Ora reached for her sunglasses and then
sighed. *As if Elizabeth couldn't recognize the car.*

"There's no law against parking in front of your old residence," Ora said aloud.

She thought of the cakes that Elizabeth used to bake her on her birthday, thick chocolate layer cakes, New York-style cheesecakes, a mousse pie one year. Well, she had the time. All that complaining about raising three kids, when she'd had lots of time. They'd spent many weekends together, before things with Robert started.

Elizabeth's hair was almost white now.

Ora glanced at herself in the rear-view mirror. She parted her short brown hair and peered at its roots. Every Monday she had it styled. Her eyelashes were still dark to their very tips, hardly needing mascara. Once she and a lover wrote personal ads for each other, for fun, and he described her eyes as smoldering. That was how she liked to think of them since, smoldering. She lowered her gaze back across the street.

"If I looked like *that* I certainly would pay someone to do something about it," she murmured. Elizabeth was weeding in the front yard, kneeling in the grass. Ora drummed her fingers on the dash. How could someone be so totally unaware of being watched, she wondered. How could that woman be so oblivious? Ora's entire body tingled when someone was watching her, as if she were charged with electricity.

Elizabeth used to warn Ora, "Be more careful." She used to say, "These aren't days when you can just go pick up men like that, Ora. Even in a small town."

"You're just paranoid because you're from New York," Ora would answer. Then, "Didn't you ever go to all those bars up there?"

"Most people don't go to places like that. Those aren't the kind of people you want to meet."

"Oh, come on," Ora said. "Then why're you always asking me to tell you about the places I go? Huh?" And they'd both laugh a little, their heads close together.

"I like . . . having them, these guys, collecting them, soaking up their . . . enthusiasm," Ora said. And then, "My new beau, Billy, is only nineteen. Where do you think he'd pick up one of those diseases you're always fretting about? I'm grabbing these guys before they've had time to become infectious."

She was trying to joke, but Elizabeth didn't even smile at that. "I think he has another side to him," she said.

"He's just a beautiful boy, is all," Ora said. "Beautiful and he moves like a devil in bed!"

"No one would ever believe such things can come out of your mouth," Elizabeth said, reddening, but she smiled too.

Once Ora thought she caught Elizabeth peering at them through a window, but it was bright outside and the light could have been playing tricks. Still, Ora felt that tingling. She could always tell.

"Not all of us are as lucky as you are," she told Elizabeth over coffee one Saturday. "Having that fine husband to provide. And kids."

"Oh, I think he runs around with his secretaries," Elizabeth said. She shrugged dismissively but her eyes reddened. Then her voice dropped to a whisper. "His father died young, you know. Some kind of early Alzheimer's or something. So it's like he has this . . . drive . . . and sometimes I think—" She exhaled and smiled. Her eyes refocused. "Ah well. I'm being silly. He's probably totally faithful. And if I ever have any proof that he's cheating I'll just shoot him to put him out of my misery."

They'd both giggled. Ora had said, "You have everything I'd want, Elizabeth. The peaceful life, no work, the wonderful kids." Elizabeth had rolled her eyes, and a few days later come knocking with the name of another young unmarried friend of Robert's, a banker, a lawyer, businessmen, newly moved to the area.

"Why, thank you kindly," Ora would say. "Tell the gentleman to call me."

"Will you be available this time? He wants to call you tonight. Will you at least give this one a chance?"

"I always give everyone a chance," Ora said. But on those occasions she'd find herself in her favorite bar in Raleigh or sneaking into fraternity parties in town. She'd change from well-tailored pastel work suits into short black skirts and chiffony tops, or denim jeans and camisoles. She'd giggle when asked to show her driver's license, getting drinks. She'd take days off from work and wave goodbye to Elizabeth from the back of Harley Davidsons. And she'd wake up in mid-afternoon or a Wednesday or Thursday, her mouth cottony, curled in a shaft of sunlight on her bed, alone. Once, but only once, she awoke with three stitches in her lower lip and a purple bruise over her left temple.

On such days she'd rise on an elbow and see Elizabeth coming toward her house, her face full of curiosity, an empty measuring cup or a full pie tin in her hand. Those days Ora ignored the doorbell.

Elizabeth unfolded her long body, pushing herself up from the ground, puffing a little as she did. She held a pile of weeds in one gloved hand, and a metal trowel in the other.

"Never worked a day in her life, that woman," Ora said aloud.

That moment, as if her soft words had pierced the glass of the windshield and shot across fifty feet, Elizabeth looked up, straight at the car. The same expression she had worn the moment Robert explained why he was leaving flickered across her face, and now as then, Ora was tempted for an instant to say, *Never mind, honey, he's just kidding, it's all a silly joke.* But then Elizabeth's eyes narrowed a little, and she did an incredible thing. She laughed. Ora leaned forward a little and lowered her window a touch. It was unmistakable. Elizabeth Engles was standing in the yard of her ex-husband's house, covered with dirt, looking like she was eighty years old, and laughing.

Through the window Ora watched Robert approach her building. His arms were empty. He walked at a leisurely pace, looking at the ground, and Ora noticed how much his hair had thinned on the top of his head. Then, abruptly, he stopped. A tinny musical note drifted up toward Ora, riding waves of Carolina jasmine-scented air. Robert pulled a small computer from his pocket, punched some keys, and then ran a hand across his face. He looked up toward Ora's window and she pressed herself against the wall, behind the curtains, continuing to watch. He glanced at his watch, turned, and went back to his car. She watched his taillights disappear into dusk.

She opened her refrigerator and glanced at the bottle of Moët that had been cooling since the previous evening. She put some champagne flutes in the freezer. She rearranged the tulip bouquet she'd bought herself on the way home, and then tried to sit in the living room by the window. She sprang up at the first sound of car tires crunching gravel. It was only a VW Rabbit belonging to her upstairs neighbor. She decided to make a date with the man who had called earlier, and riffled through her address book for his number. She left a message on his answering machine.

Finally footsteps sounded on her landing. She opened the door before the bell rang. Robert held a bouquet of red roses toward her and said, "Happy birthday, sweetheart!"

She let out a long sigh and her eyes filled.

"Oh, darling, you remembered!" she said.

"So what's for dinner?" he asked.

Her smile faded for only an instant. "You made a reservation for dinner," she said.

Robert turned on his back and flipped on a light. Ora was staring at the ceiling with tears in her eyes.

"What is it?" he asked.

"Nothing," she said.

"Are you just . . . not turned on tonight?"

"I guess that's it." She didn't say how she couldn't refrain from seeing the image of him reappearing in the restaurant, dripping wet, panic in his eyes. He'd volunteered to go get the car when the thunderstorm didn't clear, and she was waiting underneath the awning when he rushed back and cried, "It's gone! Stolen, alarm and all!" She'd run out with him, feeling the rain hammer her back and soak her sequined dress. She'd watched him careen madly toward Iredell Street.

She'd stopped, caught her breath, and lifted her face to the rain.

"Come *on*!" he yelled.

"It's the other way," she said, almost whispering.

"What do you mean?"

"We parked it down this way." And she turned the corner and there was the Mercedes, sheets of water streaming down its windshield. He'd immediately smiled and said, "Oh, how silly of me!" and she'd said, "It's all right, you have so many things on your mind these days."

They sat in the car with steam rising from their bodies, fogging the windshield and obscuring the view until Robert turned on the air conditioner. Ora shivered and finally asked him for his jacket.

"I remember everything at work," he said as he worked one arm out of a sleeve, then the other.

"Of course."

"They wouldn't pay me a six-figure salary if I didn't keep on top of things."

"I know it."

"It's just all these little insignificant things."

She sat motionless as they drove on the freeway, holding her breath as they approached each exit. Her muscles were knotted by the time they got to her own, and five hundred feet before the exit she said, "Robert, go right. We're there." He slapped the steering wheel with his open palm and said, "Damn it, I know where we are." The tires squealed as he rounded the turn.

"Why aren't you turned on?" Robert asked, following Ora's gaze up to the ceiling. "It's never been a problem before."

"Maybe we should . . . talk."

"Times were we'd go weeks without talking," he said. "You'd go wild when I walked in the door, not let me get a word out."

She ran her fingers over her breasts and down her hips, sliding them over the smooth silk of the teddy he'd brought her. The lace made her itch.

"I have a closet full of lingerie from Victoria's Secret," she said.

"You're tired of my presents?"

"I didn't say that. I just . . . I don't know."

The first box from Victoria's Secret had come in the mail, nearly four years ago, for her birthday. The card said, "From a secret admirer—just look out your window." She'd worn the black garter belt under her clothes that same night when Robert and Elizabeth came over to wish her a happy birthday. She remembered how vividly she'd felt the silk straps against her thighs while Elizabeth cut the cake she'd brought, and how Robert's hand had suddenly slid down her leg as they sat in her kitchen when Elizabeth went to get a cup of warm water in which to dip the cake knife so it wouldn't stick. Ora's whole body had warmed and that moment she mentally broke her date for later that evening with her boss's brother. That moment she looked at Robert and saw not his graying hair or leathery skin or the pouches beneath his eyes but a man who was willing to take chances. He crawled in through her side door at two A.M. that same night, and they made love in her living room, on her sofa, directly across the driveway from his and Elizabeth's bedroom.

"If you wanna talk, talk," Robert grumbled. Ora sighed.

"I saw Elizabeth today," she said, and Robert said, "You did? How did she look?"

"Oh, she's lost some weight and looked quite good."

"Really?"

She felt a mild warming. She pulled lightly at Robert's hair. "Do you think of her ever?" she asked, breathing lightly in his ear, flicking her tongue against its edge.

"Elizabeth? No."

"Never?"

"I hardly remember being married to her." He kissed her hard and thrust his tongue into her mouth but she turned her head and saw their reflection in the mirror. He didn't work out much any more and his skin was starting to hang off him a little. The hair on his chest was going white. He brushed her neck with light kisses.

After a moment she asked, "You haven't seen that girl any more, have you?"

There was a silence.

"I saw her at work," he said slowly.

She turned to him, flicked off the lights, pressed against him. "I hope you didn't talk to her, though," she said, starting to kiss him.

"Only hello."

"That's it?"

"That's all."

"Good." And she let him slide off the silk panties he'd bought her and press himself into her and shove his tongue into her mouth and she bit her lip so hard she tasted blood when he moaned, "Oh Ora, I love you, I'm going to stay with you forever."

"Your father died quite young, didn't he?" Ora asked over ham biscuits in the morning. Robert stiffened, and his nostrils flickered. "What does that have to do with anything?" he asked.

"I'm just wondering, is all. You never talk about him."

"Well, he wasn't that young when he died."

"What was he like?"

"Look, I have to get to work soon," Robert said.

"Did you two get along? Were you alike?" she asked, using her lowest, thickest voice. "I just want to know. About your kin, I mean."

"Look. This is what I was meaning to get around to last night," Robert said slowly. He didn't look at her as he spoke. "I've been thinking a lot lately, in particular about how much you mean to me."

Ora felt the biscuit stick in her throat. "Uh huh," she said.

"You know how after things happened and I wasn't sure what I wanted, you seemed so clear on wanting me to leave Elizabeth— and in all the other affairs I'd never thought of leaving her, you knew that."

"I never thought you would," she whispered.

"I did it for you, you know that."

She tried to swallow. "I just never . . . thought you would."

"Well, you got me."

She nodded. He slowly lifted his eyes to hers and smiled a tentative smile that made her wince.

"Remember how we used to talk about running away, to New York or Los Angeles or someplace like that, you and me, for weeks, maybe forever, without anyone knowing where we were?" Ora whispered.

"We did?"

"Uh huh." She cupped her hand over his. "And Europe, and Africa. Just stealing away, making love in the Vatican maybe. There your divorce doesn't even count."

"Well, now I'm ready for a lot more than that, baby."

Her hands went cold. "More?" she said.

He glanced at his watch.

"You know—marriage and all that."

The room shivered a little. Ora got up to close a window, then put another kettle on the stove. Robert rose and put his arms around her, pressing himself into her back She felt him starting to get an erection against her buttocks.

"What do you think, Ora honey? You want to do it?"

"My goodness," she whispered.

He turned her toward him and lifted her hand a little and then bent down to kiss it lightly.

"I don't have the ring yet, and I suppose I should have waited until then, but at our age—"

"Our age!" she said. Still she couldn't talk aloud, but she raised her eyes and batted her eyelashes and managed a smile as she said, "Remember, I'm fifteen years younger and I've never gotten a ring!"

"Right—of course," he said. He seemed to be shouting by comparison. "I'll get one right away. Tonight. Does that mean—oh honey, there's no reason to cry!"

"Yes, of course," she said.

"You'll marry me?"

"Yes; yes."

"Don't cry," he said again. "I'll make sure I get you your ring immediately. We can buy another house and you'll forget all about the one you had to sell. And I'll get you the biggest diamond you've ever seen, much bigger than Elizabeth's. I was only starting out then; now I can get a rock."

"Yes."

He flipped open his pocket computer and tapped in a note, then closed it and was gone.

She watched him through her window, watched him thread his way to his Mercedes with its crumpled left front fender. She recalled the rush she'd felt in the moment she had reached over and without thinking, without really knowing what she would do next, yanked the wheel as hard as she could to the right and then felt him over-compensate to the left. Now, she watched him put on his seatbelt, look over his shoulder, back out. If she'd been wearing a seatbelt the day of their accident, she might not have gotten her face slashed. She ran her finger down the sutures and went to look in the mirror. They had told her the silk had to stay in place a few days, to prevent scarring. With a small pair of nail scissors and her eyebrow tweezers, she worked the stitches loose. She touched her skin again, and wondered what kind of mark she would add to her collection.

In the afternoon Ora dropped the champagne her boss had given her onto her sofa and stripped off her cream linen suit, her white stockings, her lace underwear. She slid the tenderloin into the oven to start it roasting while she showered. She shaved her legs and rubbed lotion all over her body and misted herself with cologne. Then she stepped into a black fitted slip of a dress with a sequined bodice.

She examined her eyes in the mirror of her vanity. They looked dull.

"It's the luster fading from this old piece-of-crap mirror," she said aloud. The vanity had belonged to her great-grandmother, and although Ora never liked it she had carted it around from her adolescent bedroom to her college dorm to her house to this apartment, because it had been specifically willed to her. The silver had blackened in spots, and many of the drawers lacked handles.

"All new furniture when we get married," she said to her reflection. "New everything."

The phone rang and she heard her mother say, "How's next week, for dress shopping?"

"Fine, Mama," Ora said.

"Great. I'll make some calls. And by the way, I talked to him. He sounds impressive."

"To Robert?"

"I called him at work. You know, introduce myself, welcome him into the family."

"Mama!"

"I told him it wasn't too late for you and he agreed."

"Agreed?"

"About children. He said, 'Anything she wants.' I like that. Oh—and he got his secretary to get the ring already. One point six carats, imagine!"

"Better not have been *Jenny*."

"He said Esther. It's a good sign when a man recognizes he needs a woman's opinion in these matters."

"Right," Ora said. She was remembering that Esther was nearly sixty, and surprised that she was still thinking of such things.

"Honey." Her mother paused. "I'm so happy for you. You finally did it, like you always wanted. It must be a great feeling."

Ora put on a pot of coffee and slid her boss's champagne into the refrigerator. She checked on the roast and went back into her bedroom, and sat in front of her vanity inspecting herself. She mentally catalogued all she would have, the house she wanted, her ring. Her boss had been so upset when she gave him two weeks' notice. She could even hire a full-time nurse to live in and help with things if it got to that.

The phone rang, but Ora let the machine pick up. It was Robert saying he'd be fifteen minutes late.

And before the message ended, Ora sprang from her seat and pulled her matching leather suitcases from under her bed and began packing her jewelry and then her black dresses and her jeans. By the time she turned to the pastel suits there was barely any room left. She checked the roast a final time, moved her tulips from her nightstand to her dining room table, glanced around the room, put on lipstick.

In the parking lot she sat with the engine running and the lights turned off. She heard through her open window, "Ora?"

The crickets chirped.

"Ora, where the hell are you?"

There was a new moon and the night was completely black.

"Ora, I'm tired and hungry and I don't have time for games!"

The scent of Carolina honeysuckle was smothering.

Ora glanced at her speedometer but maintained her eighty-mile-an-hour pace. She liked the feel of a hundred-and-forty horsepower barreling her along in the dark. Every so often the car veered a little as she leaned forward and looked out at the stars. The road was empty, so no one honked at her. Although she was breathing rapidly, she concentrated on inhaling deeply. The night air was scented with pine and clover out here. Her highbeams lit a path for her beneath the loblollies that bordered the interstate.

Her headlights picked out a figure by the side of the road, and she slowed. She could make out a young bearded man, thirty perhaps, in tight jeans and a black jacket. He had his thumb out, and for a moment her heart pounded in her ribcage in a familiar way. Running her tongue over her upper lip she could taste the flowery scent of the bright red lipstick she'd put on and she felt a tingling, a breathlessness, in her middle. But then she dropped her foot back onto the accelerator and he slid past her on the highway, thumb out, not even meeting her eye, growing steadily smaller in the rear-view mirror. She flipped through the stations on the radio until she found some country she liked, and her heart, instead of slowing, swelled within her and she let herself sing aloud to the music.

I'M DEEPLY GRATEFUL to many whose support over the years has enriched and sustained my writing: Sorin Iarovici, Virginia Holman, Gene Langston, Darcy Jacobs, Robin Farabaugh, and Ranjini Phillips. The title story benefited from the wisdom of my workshop colleagues at the wonderful Sewanee Writers' Conference. A Durham Arts Council Emerging Artist Grant and the Aspen Writers' Foundation fueled my momentum. I am lucky to have Amy Rogers and Frye Gaillard as editors. Thanks to Shawnta Wright for helping me carve out time. And finally, heartfelt thanks to Ariel and Justin for helping me keep sight of what really matters.

Novello Festival Press

Novello Festival Press, under the auspices of the Public Library of Charlotte and Mecklenburg County and through the publication of books of literary excellence, enhances the awareness of the literary arts, helps discover and nurture new literary talent, celebrates the rich diversity of the human experience, and expands the opportunities for writers and readers from within our community and its surrounding geographic region.

The Public Library of Charlotte and Mecklenburg County

For more than a century, the Public Library of Charlotte and Mecklenburg County has provided essential community service and out-reach to the citizens of the Charlotte area. Today, it is one of the premier libraries in the country—named "Library of the Year" and "Library of the Future" in the 1990s—with 23 branches, 1.6 million volumes, 20,000 videos and DVDs, 9,000 maps and 8,000 compact discs. The Library also sponsors a number of community-based programs, from the award-winning Novello Festival of Reading, a celebration that accentuates the fun of reading and learning, to branch programs for young people and adults.

This project received support from the North Carolina Arts Council, an agency funded by the State of North Carolina and the National Endowment for the Arts.